Booked For The Winter

JOCELYNE SOTO

Booked
For the Winter

When it came to certain things in life, I didn't know much, beyond what I was taught by my mother.

I didn't know just how big and different things were outside of that—until I decided to move somewhere new and got a job at a bookstore.

Being surrounded by stories left and right made me realize my life had been sheltered.

But it wasn't only the books that opened my mind—the bookstore owners helped too.

Two very hot, older-than-me bookstore owners.

They helped open my eyes to the differences in the world… including how it feels to belong to two.

They are hot as sin, and did I mention they're twins?

They are showing me just how good things can be.

This book touches upon the subject of multiple partners at the same time. There are sexually explicit scenes as well as foul language involved.

If this is not something you are comfortable with, please do not read on.

Thank you.

PROLOGUE

ZOEY

It's majestic.

There's greenery everywhere, capped with snow waiting to be melted by the sun. If my face wasn't pressed against the bus window, I would have thought I was watching a movie.

Everything just looks so beautiful, so perfect. I can't help but proudly smile at myself a bit for choosing this place. Had I listened to my mom, I wouldn't have seen the beauty before me now.

"You can't go out in the world by yourself, Zoey. It's too big and too dangerous. You have to stay here, where you are safe. You have to remember that."

That has been drilled into my mind ever since I can remember. A day wouldn't go by when I wouldn't hear it from my mom.

We would be sitting at the dining room table, and she

would go on a tangent, talking for a good half hour about how the world we live in is a terrifying place.

She was right, to a certain extent.

The world is a terrifying place, especially when you start to wander through it without a single idea of where you're going or who you might meet.

Yes, there are some parts of the world that are ugly and people walking through life who are evil, but that doesn't mean everything is that way.

"Crystal Springs approaching. This will be the final stop." The bus automated announcement comes through, and I can't help but sit up straight in my seat.

This is it.

After seventy hours on multiple buses across the country, I've finally made it. There were a few times I thought I would never see the end, but here we are, and it's the most beautiful end I could have imagined.

When I picked the most random, furthest from home destination, I thought I was going to end up somewhere I would want to leave right away. I expected it to be dingy, with no life, but as the bus driver takes us closer to the lakefront town I chose, I know I won't want to leave.

When the town comes into view, and I take in everything I can, I think I start to fall in love.

Through movies and television shows, I learned California was beautiful, but I always thought that only applied to the beach and the coast. From what I can see now, though, the beauty of it all extends to the mountains too.

The town of Crystal Springs is small and quaint but full of life. There are people walking around, laughing and enjoying their days. There are cute storefronts I can't wait to shop at and restaurants I can't wait to try.

This is definitely a change from where I grew up in West Virginia, but as I watch through my window, I think I will be more than okay with that change.

When the driver pulls up to the bus terminal, the excitement rolls through my body and has me jumping a little in my seat.

The second I step off the bus and breathe in the fresh air, any nerves I felt about moving across the country by myself start to fade.

As I walk away from the bus that took me from everything I knew and head into town, my mother's words swim through my mind.

This world is a dangerous place, as she told me countless times, but knowing that isn't going to stop me from exploring it.

I love my mother, I do, but she's not always right and not what someone would call a reliable source of information. She spent the majority of her life living in a religious commune, and after leaving, she landed in a cult.

She walked away from the cult when I was two, and from there, instead of forging her own path in life, she held tight to what she learned.

She raised me to believe everyone who did things a smidge different than us was evil. If someone wore jeans, anything with glitter, or even graphic tees, they were the devil's children. If they had tattoos or ear piercings, they had to be to be rebelling against their parents.

I believed every word she said and she used it to keep me in line, to make sure I never veered off more than five feet from her. It wasn't until I was eighteen that I realized just how sheltered my life had been, just how small my perspective was, how much she exaggerated to scare me.

Yes, everything is just as my mother told me it would be.

Terrifying.

Strange.

Scary.

Of course, there are a few things that have me looking over my shoulder as I make my way to where I need to go. The nerves I thought started to fade away swirl again, and for a second, I start to regret my decision.

That feeling intensifies when I meet with the property manager I've been in contact with for an apartment.

Did I make a mistake?

Am I being irrational?

I've never done anything like this, and as the property manager walks me to the apartment I put a down payment on, the one in the middle of town, furnished but sight-unseen, I start to think I was crazy for deciding to come to a place I only know through an internet search.

But then I walked inside.

Seeing the mountains topped with snow and the massive lake that is the town's namesake has me feeling better about my decision.

This is my home now, and this apartment is my safe haven. It will be scary, of course, but with time, I'm sure it'll be the best decision I've ever made.

* * *

IT DOESN'T TAKE ME LONG TO GET SETTLED. I DIDN'T BRING much with me to begin with, but it does take me a few days to work up the courage to go out and explore my new home outside of going to the grocery store.

When I finally venture out, I fall in love with everything I see.

The town looks to be a staple for tourists, but it still feels homey. There isn't a whole lot of noise, which I like.

This place has a lot to offer.

Down the street from where I live is a little bookstore that seems warm and welcoming, but I have yet to step foot inside.

From what I can see, the store gets the occasional customer during the day, but it's not overly busy. I did notice two men come and go from the store all time.

Two men who look alike. Twins, if I had to guess.

One has hair that covers his ears; the other has his hair buzzed.

Even though I haven't made my way inside, it feels like I know this store already.

Today, I'm making it my mission to walk in—not only to see if the bookstore will be my second safe haven, but also to work up the courage to ask for a job.

The money I had when I left West Virginia is slowly decreasing, and I need to do something to bring money in.

The bookstore seems like a good choice.

Since this is a tourist town, I'm sure once the snow sticks to the mountain for the winter months, the store will be filled with costumers, and they will need help.

The only way to find out is if I open the door and walk in.

So, that's what I do.

With my shoulders pushed back and a deep breath, I walk in.

The bell dings, and I come face to face with two of the most beautiful men I have ever seen.

I think I forget how to breathe for a second as I stare at the man behind the counter, but I'm able to compose myself just enough and give him a small smile.

But that's all I'm able to do. I can't find it in me to open my mouth and introduce myself or ask for a job.

Nope; instead, I just walk deeper into the store and lose myself within the stories.

CHAPTER 1

MATIAS

 don't know what I did in a past life, but I'm currently being tortured for my sins. I just know I am. There is no other reason for me to be going through this hell.

Did I tie someone to a chair and make them bleed because they crossed me?

Did one of my past selves murder someone?

Was a library book checked out and never turned back in?

Why oh fucking why am I getting tortured right now? I don't fucking deserve this.

I hear the floorboards at the back of the store creak, and I can't help but drop my head down to my chest.

Three weeks.

For three weeks, I have been suffering, tortured, battling with my inner self to not find the source and see the sight up close.

And what a sight it is.

I first laid my eyes on her one quiet Sunday three weeks ago.

Fucking beautiful.

That day is embedded into my mind.

The bell above the door rang while I was behind the computer, inputting inventory. When I looked up, all I could see was a blonde-haired beauty with doe eyes filled with wonder.

She came in with what looked like determination on her face. I thought she was going to ask me something, but instead, she gave me a small smile and wandered deeper into the bookstore.

Her appearance left me dumbfounded. As she walked away, I was left at the counter, not being able to say a word. She affected me that damn much.

Instead of following behind her, I shook my head and went back to work, doing everything possible to get my head in the right place.

It had worked—so much so, I thought she had left when I was in the back room or something. Then, fifteen minutes before closing, she appeared yet again and left without saying a word, awarding me with another smile.

That night, I spent hours thinking about her. She was in my head so much that by the time I had gone to sleep, I was starting to think I had made her up. But the next morning, the door to the shop opened once more, and there she was.

Once again, she came in looking like she wanted to ask something but didn't, instead giving me a smile and walking to the back of the store.

She came back the next day and has repeated the pattern for three weeks.

Every day, thirty minutes after we open, my mysterious girl walks in, stays until about noon, and then comes back until fifteen minutes before closing.

The first few days, she went to the same section, and then she ventured out. Every day, though, there's a new book in her hands.

To say I'm intrigued by her would be an understatement.

Most days, I go about my business, working and acting as if she isn't in my store.

It works, mostly, but only about eighty five percent of the time. The other fifteen percent has me wondering who she is, where she came from, and why she has decided to come into my bookstore, of all places, day after day.

Not just your bookstore.

Right. I almost forgot I share the place.

About ten years ago, after selling a tech start-up to some tech genius in Silicon Valley, my twin brother, Samuel, and I decided to move to the lakefront town of Crystal Springs.

We spent the better part of our childhood here before our parents moved our family to New York City, so when we came into our money, we decided on a place where we could settle down a bit, away from all the noise living in a big city could bring. For about a year, Crystal Springs was just a home base, a place we could come back to after we traveled somewhere else. Eventually, we became a part of the community, and after about a year, we decided to contribute to the town in some way.

That's when the idea of a bookstore came about. At the time, it sounded a bit unprecedented, since we knew nothing about running a retail business, let alone a bookstore, but we decided to take a chance and build a place where people, those from Crystal Springs and beyond, could come to find an escape, fictional or otherwise.

Now, at the age of thirty-three, we live in a small mountain town and run a successful bookstore. It helps somewhat that we are the only bookstore in a hundred miles.

I'm not going to lie—when my broody, hard-to-comprehend brother suggested we open a bookstore, I was floored. Never in my wildest dreams did I think those words would come out of his mouth, but they did, and somehow, I agreed.

Not for one second do I regret the decision. Moving to Crystal Springs has offered us the seclusion we desired so much.

The one thing moving to a mountain town has not offered us? Women.

In our ten or so years living here, there have been a handful of women who have caught our eye. Most have been locals who have been here their whole lives or moved back after a few years away. Others have been tourists wanting to get their hands on a cock that will make them forget about their lives back home.

New women don't cross our paths very often, but when they do, we make the most of it.

And when I say we, I do, in fact, mean we. The bookstore isn't the only thing my brother and I share. We share women too.

We don't share all our women, but when the opportunity presents itself, we take it.

There's just something about sharing a woman, the look of lust in her eyes when I'm pounding into her pussy while she swallows down another cock, has me hard behind the zipper of my jeans.

Readjusting myself, I try to clear my head and go back to finishing my inventory for the week. We are running low on a few titles, and I need to know how many copies we need to order.

As I'm scanning barcodes, my mind goes to the doe eyed blonde who is currently somewhere in the store, and I can't help but to wonder if she likes to be shared.

I can't help but kick myself in the ass for letting my mind go in that direction.

It's wrong, especially since she appears to be so damn young, but apparently, I can't help myself. She has taken over my mind.

There's a reason why I'm always at the checkout counter whenever she arrives—so my eyes can roam every inch of her that I can.

From what I've noticed, apart from beautiful eyes and golden blonde hair that shines in the sunlight, she has full breasts she hides in oversized sweaters and a beautifully rounded ass that would fit perfectly in my hands.

The image of her ass filling my hands as I pound into her fills my mind, and, fuck, my mouth waters at the thought.

I bet she would look so good bent over one of the chairs we have in the back.

"Why are you fucking drooling?" A voice much like my own takes me out of my fantasy. And such a good fantasy it was.

I turn to my twin brother and give him my best smirk. "Wouldn't you like to know?" I say with a wink. He knows me well enough to know when I have sex on the brain, and he rolls his eyes.

"Let me guess—it has to do with the diablilla currently curled up in the reading chair in the back?" he says, raising an eyebrow at me and taking the inventory clipboard I have in my hand, checking to see where I left off.

I can't help but smirk at him calling our repeat customer a little devil. That's exactly what she is.

"She's caught your eye too?" I ask, my smirk taking on a life of its own. Thoughts of her being shared by us run rampant in my mind.

"It's a little hard not to notice her, what with her coming in here every day. She has to be new into town."

"She has to be. No tourist stays this long," I muse. It's a good thing we're in our stockroom; otherwise, she would be able to hear us.

"I was thinking about offering her a job," Sam says, taking me by surprise.

"Do we need another employee?" I ask, almost thrown by his suggestion. He doesn't usually hire people. I do.

Our bookstore is a decent size, but it's not really a place that needs more than two people to run it on any given day. Sure, when we get busy, especially during peak seasons, we have staff, but the majority of the time, it's just us. That has been fine up until now.

"It would be nice to have someone else in this place." He shrugs as he speaks. "Seeing your face 24/7 gets a little old. Besides, its December. People will start making their way into town to have a snowy Christmas. The more hands we have to help the better. "

I narrow my eyes at him.

This fucker.

He has the same face I do, minus the facial hair. Seeing his face 24/7 is getting old, not the other way around.

But he does have a point. The two of us spend way too much fucking time together. It would be good to have someone else in the mix. Besides, our other staff isn't expected to come in until a week and a half before Christmas.

"Okay, but we don't know if she's a tourist on an extended vacation. Offering a job could be pointless."

Sam is already shaking his head before I finish speaking. "From what I've heard, she moved here a few days before she started coming in. Apparently, she's renting a place over at the Munzer building."

I would say I'm impressed, but living in a town this size, news travels fast, especially when it has to do with new people.

I take a second to think about my brother's idea. It would be nice to have someone else to talk to as we wait for the busy season.

"You really want to offer her a job?" I ask.

He nods without any hesitation. "I do."

"Okay then. Let's go talk to her."

Why do I get a feeling this might just be one of the best ideas my brother has ever had?

CHAPTER 2

Samuel

I'm not usually one to suggest we hire someone.

That's usually Matias' job. He's the more personable and charismatic one out of the two of us and tends to see when someone will like working here or not. I tend to stay away from that type of thing and instead concentrate on the back end, bringing in inventory and handling the financial stuff.

But what my brother doesn't know is the woman I want to offer a job has captivated me since the moment I saw her get off the Greyhound all those weeks ago.

I had just left the bookstore for the day and decided to grab something to eat before I headed up to the cabin. The bus had pulled up to the terminal as I was crossing the street, and once I made it to the other side, I caught a glimpse of a breathtaking woman with blonde hair to her shoulders, her doe eyes wide with excitement.

Something about her made me stop.

Never has a woman caught my eye quite like her.

She was young, she looked innocent, and all I wanted to was to touch her to see if she was real.

Of course, I held back, but that didn't stop me from seeing where she was heading.

I had no reason to follow her, even if I told myself I was only doing it because she might need guidance. I did realize I was acting like a stalker about five minutes in, though, so when she turned the corner I stopped myself and went to get my dinner.

I thought about her that night, thought about how it would have felt to touch her, to feel her body against mine. I had only seen her for a few minutes, but that was enough for my mind to conjure up images of her while I stroked my cock.

Images of her on her knees in front of me, swallowing every last inch. Thoughts of how tight her little cunt would feel wrapped around me.

It worked, because I came damn hard for this strange woman.

It makes me demented, I know.

Now imagine my surprise when I went to work the next day and saw her there, curled up in one of the shop's reading chairs. I wanted to approach her, but I controlled myself and kept my distance.

For the next three weeks, I stayed away, watching her whenever I had a chance.

I'm not going to lie and say my thoughts haven't been dirty these last three weeks. They most certainly have.

There have been thoughts about bending her over the arm of the chair she always sits in and fucking her until her legs give out. When I noticed Matias looking at her a certain type of way a few days in, I started picturing her taking both of us, imagining how beautiful she would look while she choked on my cock as Matias pounded her tight little pussy.

Fuck; if those thoughts don't make me hard, I don't know what else will.

I fear, though, my thoughts and fantasies about this woman are why I told my brother I was thinking about hiring her.

We are set with employees for when the snow sticks in a week or two and tourist start to flock in.

My mind was clouded with fake images of her on her knees, taking us both.

Granted, it would be nice to add someone else to the list of people I can talk to who isn't my brother.

I already look like the man, we live in the same house, and on top of working together, sometimes, it's nice to speak to people that aren't him.

It was no surprise whatsoever when he agreed to offer her a job.

With a nod at his suggestion to talk to the girl, we leave the stock room and head to where she's sitting.

For three weeks, she has taken to a chair in a dark corner of the store. She reads all day, only leaving around lunchtime and coming back shortly after. Every day, it's always that damn chair.

The only reason we have chairs in the first place is because Sonia, the older lady who runs the one of the inns down the street, gave them to us when we first opened. They're an eye sore, but they're definitely comfortable and add a homey feeling to the place.

We approach the back corner, and there she is, all curled up with a book from the fantasy section.

I've noticed she doesn't read one set genre. She's all over the place. Maybe she's discovering what she likes.

She looks beautiful, though.

Her blonde hair is up, a mess on top of her head. She's wearing a hoodie that is way too big for her, and her bottom lip is between her teeth.

What I wouldn't give to be able to pull that lip free and take it between my teeth, give it a good suck.

Or see those lips wrapped around my cock.

Matias has to know what I'm thinking, because he stabs his elbow into my side.

Right.

Focus, Samuel.

I clear my throat and get her attention right away. In this day and age, I'm surprised she doesn't have earbuds in.

"Hello," I say, sounding awkward as fuck.

She sits up, closing the book and placing it on her lap.

As she looks up at us, her eyes go a little wide with a little bit of fear.

"Hi," she says on a whisper as her eyes bounce between me and Matias.

At times, people they can't tell us a part—same height, same build, same eye color. The only visible difference to them is Matias has longish hair and a beard and I don't. My hair is buzzed and I hate the feeling of a facial hair. That is true, but once someone gets to know us on a personal level, they start to learn we are two completely different people.

Matias is more outgoing and a social butterfly. I, on the

other hand, am a brooding bastard who grunts a lot. My brother's words, not mine.

But I guess that's what happens when your parents are socialites for a living—you become a broody bastard.

I shake the thought of my parents and my brooding tendencies out of my head and concentrate back on the girl.

"Did I do something wrong? Was I disturbing the peas or something?" she asks, her eyes wide.

I haven't heard this girl speak a single time, and she somehow thinks she's a disturbance?

"You would have to make some kind of noise to be a disturbance," Matias says, and I don't have to turn to face him to see his smirk. I can hear it in his voice.

The girl's face turns a light shade of red, embarrassed by his comment.

"Right." She nods. "I just thought I was taking up too much space or you wanted your chair back." She gives us a small smile.

"Trust us, you can take up all the space you want," my brother muses, and I fight the urge to stab him in the ribs. He's talking like a damn teenager trying to get his dick wet for the first time instead of a grown man.

And he says *he's* the mature one.

One day, I'm going to record his ass so he can see what he's really like.

The woman in front of us blushes.

Since this feels like it's not going anywhere, I clear my throat and intervene. "What's your name, cariño?"

At the word cariño, her doe eyes turn to me, and I swear, I see her lick her lips.

I'm just as bad as my brother.

"Zoey," she breathes out.

Zoey.

A beautiful name for a beautiful girl.

I read somewhere that it means life, and I take more of her in. The name fits her perfectly. Her eyes shine bright with life, and I have a feeling nothing can dull it.

"Zoey, it's nice to meet you. I'm Samuel, and this is my brother Matias. We own the bookstore."

Her smile grows a bit, and she gives a small wave. "It's nice to meet you both."

There's a pause for a moment before my brother starts talking. "We wanted to come talk to you about a possible offer," Matias says to her.

This makes her sit up a little straighter, and her eyebrows bunch up a little bit.

"An offer? What kind of offer?" Her voice has some reservation to it, and honestly, mine would too if two fucking strangers approached me with an offer.

She probably thinks we're going to ask to sleep with her.

To make things less weird, I intervene.

"We would like to offer you a job, if you're interested," I say, throwing her a smile to make this more comfortable.

"A job?" she asks with a bit of relief in her voice.

"Yes. We could use an extra hand. That is, if you will be in town for a while," Matias answers back.

This is a thing we do, talk back and forth. We have been doing it since we were kids.

"I will be." She nods enthusiastically. "I will be here for a while. I was actually going to ask if you were hiring the first day I came in here, but I chickened out. I figured since winter was here you might need more help," she says, a small blush covering her cheeks.

I give Zoey a reassuring smile.

"Well, if you need the job, it's yours. It's fairly simple, just stocking the shelves and pointing the occasional customer in the right direction. One or both of us will be here all the time, and it would be nice to have another face around the store."

She doesn't say anything for a solid minute; she just continues to look between me and Matias.

Does she think we're a bunch of creeps?

We have to be, because who else approaches a young girl in a bookstore to offer her a job? We should have waited for her to work up the courage to come to us. For a few seconds, I start to think she may say no.

Which is why, when she finally speaks, she takes me by surprise.

"When can I start?"

CHAPTER 3

Zoey

$\mathcal{I}$mpulsive.

That's the word my mom would use to describe my actions. She would say I'm an impulsive girl who doesn't take anything, including her plans, into consideration.

Then, she would tell me I should think long and hard before I say or do anything.

She told me I was impulsive moving to California, and she would say the same thing about me taking a job from to individual, two men, I barely even know.

But isn't that how job interviews work?

You talk to a stranger for a few minutes and then get offered the job?

I wouldn't call these men strangers, though. They're two strangers I've very discreetly spent the past three weeks with —in a non-creepy way.

Well, maybe a little creepy.

I was hanging out in the back of their store, hearing their conversation, aware of their every move.

I could have avoided all this creepiness if I had just introduced myself when I first walked in, but when I came face to face with the most gorgeous man I have ever laid eyes on, I nearly melted.

Not only was he gorgeous, the man was hot beyond measure. Butterflies took flight all over my insides. I wanted to see if he was real, to reach out and touch his beard to see if it was soft.

I wanted to do a lot of things, but I refrained. I probably seemed weird; I didn't want to come off as crazy too.

So instead of drooling over this man in the middle of the store, I went to the furthest shelf I could see and ended up settling into a chair in the back with a book from the murder mystery section.

The book captivated me, sucking me in until the world around me was invisible.

Well, nearly.

The only thing that grabbed my attention more than the book was the handsome man. Every time he passed me, he would smile, and with every smile, I'd blush.

He was older than me, possibly in his thirties, and he most likely thought I was just a kid trying to escape life.

I was, but he didn't know that exactly.

That day, I read the book and returned his smile every chance I could, creating a cycle when I came back the next day and did the same.

It was a few days in that I had a run in with his twin.

When I walked in that morning, I had seen the man I now know as Matias up front, opening a few boxes. His hair looked like he had just rolled of bed, and for some reason, I took notice. So, when I saw him a few hours later and noticed he suddenly had a buzz cut, it threw me for a loop. It took me a few seconds to remember I had seen twins coming in and out of this place.

Like when I saw his brother, butterflies started to form in my stomach, so I did what I did best: I smiled and walked to the back.

I ended up hanging out at the store nearly every day for three weeks. The only days I would stay home was when the store was closed.

Did I have a reason for spending so much time there?

Not really, I could have spent time at the Mexican bakery down the street or even at the marina, but something about the store called to me.

I want to say it was the books, all the stories behind the covers, but I think it was also the two men who had my stomach doing summersaults.

The more time I spent in the store, the more I learned about all these new places, fictional and not—and about the two people who ran the place.

I won't ever admit it, but I leaned their names before they introduced themselves.

Matias is more talkative while Samuel is quieter.

Both brothers are equally as gorgeous and manly, but they do have their distinctions.

Sam, as I heard his brother call him, doesn't have a beard and has a swagger to him that silently says not to mess with him.

Matias is the brother who keeps his hair longer and beard short. He's a go with the flow guy, but he also has a bad-boy feel to him. He's the type of man my mother told me to stay away from.

Both men have my attention; they make me feel something I have never felt before, this discomfort that I can't get rid of.

That feeling became more apparent when they approached me and offered me a job. I thought once they spoke to me, that feeling would go away, but I was wrong.

Having their words directed at me made me more self-conscious. Everything about them made me more aware of myself.

I liked the feeling.

A lot.

So, I accepted the job.

Now, here I am, about to start my first day of real work, and I'm a nervous mess.

Before opening the door, I take a deep breath and center myself.

I can do this. I can spend eight glorious hours around these men and not make a mockery of myself. I can do this.

Once I'm completely centered, I pull the door open and inhale the lovely scent of books.

Never did I think I would like this scent as much as I do. Growing up, I wasn't much of a reader, I guess because my mother never let me—the devil's work, she called it.

The first time I walked in here, I didn't know what to expect, but I was captivated from the jump.

I love it, and now, I'm going to work in a book lover's dream.

Well, a book lover's dream and maybe my own fantasy.

"Good morning," I say, finding the two brothers standing at the counter.

They look so hot. Both of them have this rugged look; I have to wonder if they're taken. If they're not, how could that be possible?

"Good morning, Zoey," Samuel says, and I'm blushing just from the sound of my name leaving his mouth.

"How are you?" Matias asks before I can answer his brother.

"Pretty good. Excited to get to work." I give them a smile that actually reaches my eyes as I close the distance.

"That's good. Ever work retail before?" Matias asks, and I shake my head.

"How old are you?" Samuel asks, not in a bad tone but more out of curiosity.

"Twenty-one," I answer.

"And have you worked at all before?" Matias asks.

I cringe a little. "Does babysitting count?"

That's the only thing my mom let me do, and even then, that was restricted to a few hours some afternoons.

A reassuring smile comes my way from Matias. "We will teach you everything you need to know."

I nod, and Samuel tells me to follow him as he walks to the stockroom. Once in there, he shows me what I need to know, and I try to digest as much as I can.

As I learn, I can't help but wish one of these two men could show me more than what it takes to run a bookstore.

I mentally kick myself at that, though, because it definitely has a sexual overtone. These men are my bosses. I shouldn't be thinking about them like that.

I shouldn't, but I will.

There is no doubt in my mind—I'm going to hell for it.

MATIAS

*M*oonlight.

Sunshine.

Vanilla.

Those are the things I think of whenever I see Zoey at the shop, the things I smell when she passes by. The things that make my cock rock hard.

I think Sam was trying to give me permanent blue balls when he thought up the idea of hiring her.

That man is fucking sadistic. He is torturing me, putting the woman I want to see naked in front of me when I can't touch her or find out if she tastes as sweet as she looks.

Fucking asshole.

He's probably struggling with this decision too. I've caught him a few times staring at her ass and looking down her shirt when he thinks nobody is looking. I know he wants her, but if I can't have her, neither can he.

That's what he fucking gets for putting us in this position.

"Do you guys really sell this many romance books?" Zoey's voice brings me back, away from thoughts of torturing my brother.

Zoey and I are stocking some of the shelves after a weekend rush. I'm working on the young adult section, and I guess she got the romance box.

It's interesting what you learn about books when you're surrounded by them all day. It's also interesting to see what people gravitate towards. They get no judgment from me, but it *is* an interesting sight.

"It's our best-selling genre. I was a little surprised by it at the beginning, but I've come to learn it's popular, and people of all kinds—including men—pick them up."

I've picked up a few myself. There's something about a romance book that quiets things down. I don't have to think; I just get lost in the pages. Do I also read romance for other reasons? Sure. Romance books are hot as fuck.

"Really?" she asks.

I turn to look her—she's busy reading the synopsis on the back of a book.

"Yeah, they are a hot seller, pun intended," I say as I slide a few books in their places. When I look back at her, she still has the book in her hands, her eyes filled with curiosity. "You should read it, see if you like it," I suggest.

She gives me a sly smile before biting her lip. "I think I will."

Fuck. She's hot, and she doesn't even know it.

I have to stop thinking about her like that. She's twenty-one, *my employee,* and I have no business even flirting with her.

But apparently, I don't care, because I abandon the books I'm shelving. Keeping my eyes on her, I reach up and grab the one book she should definitely read, handing it over with a smile.

"You should start with this one. It's a little tamer than most, but the way the author tackles the more explicit scenes makes it one of my favorites."

Her eyes go wide as she takes the book and digests my words.

"You've read this one?" she asks, her voice breaking a little.

I step closer to her, leaning in as much as possible without touching her. "I did. I can show you the parts I enjoyed if you like."

I feel her shiver and this time she's the one stepping closer to me.

"I would like that." I swear, I can feel her breath on my skin as she says the words.

"How would you like me to do that? I can tell you the pages, or I could just show you?" I lean my mouth even closer, my lips nearly touching her ear.

I can smell her sweetness, can practically taste it.

"Show me how?" she breathes out, her voice full of lust.

I lean back somewhat, enough to see her face, and place a hand against her cheek, caressing her delicate skin with my thumb.

"Show you the exact pages. Or, if you're interested, I can show you what happens in the scenes."

She nearly whispers her next words. "And if choose the latter? What would happen then?"

My thumb travels to her lips and slowly map them out.

"I would give you a choice. There are two scenes in this

book that caught my attention. In one, he used his hands, and in the other, he used his mouth."

She leans deeper into my touch, her bottom lip between her teeth.

"And if I said I wanted you to show me what happens when he uses his hand? What would you do then?" She swallows hard, but when she looks up at me with those blue eyes, I nearly crumble. It doesn't help that she leans more into my touch while her own hands start making their way up my chest.

Fuck. This is happening. This is really happening. I should stop this before I regret it, before we *both* regret it. She's my employee now, not some random woman in town for the weekend. I keep telling myself that, but I can't seem to stop the words.

"Then, if I had your permission, I would move my hand down," I say, and when she nods, I move the hand on her cheek down her body. I run my fingers over her neck to her chest covered by her V-neck shirt.

"Then what?" she asks. I see her chest moving up and down.

"Then, I would touch you here," I lean forward and place my lips just under her ear and kiss her, all while my hand moves to her chest, circling my fingertip around the edge of her tit.

"I would rub you like this." I run my fingers against her skin, rub little circles around her nipples, feel them harden through the fabric.

"What would you do next?"

"Then my hand would go down like this." I run my hands down her body, feeling her curves. I wish she wasn't clothed so I could feel her skin against mine. "Once I reach your hips, my hand would go here." I slide my hand further, past the waist band of her jeans, and press against her pussy.

I can feel her heat through the material.

"Do you think I could buy this so I could read it?"

"What?" I breathe against her skin.

"Can I buy the book?" she says. Her voice isn't as breathless as it was just a few seconds ago.

I pull back, and she's looking at me with those big doe eyes. The book I handed her is in her hand, and she is standing a few feet from me.

Is my imagination playing tricks on me?

Was I not touching her?

Fucking hell. I need to get this girl out of my head somehow, because being around her is going to drive me crazy.

I clear my throat and readjust myself as discreetly as possible.

"Yeah." I clear my throat again. "Yeah, you can buy it. Buy any book you want."

She lets out a little giggle and then gives me a kiss on the cheek.

"Thank you," she says before slipping away to the front of the store.

"Fuck." I abandon the books and head to the back.

I need to find my brother and kick his ass for putting temptation in front of me.

That fucking bastard.

CHAPTER 5

SAMUEL

*M*at most likely hates me.

I've been leaving him to handle the bookstore and training Zoey, all while I work from home.

I'm an asshole, I know. I knew I was an asshole when he came home a few days ago, grumbling about him going crazy, before disappearing upstairs.

I'm a bigger asshole now, because I left the store early to go down to the town bar. I couldn't spend another second with her, fighting the urge to touch her.

Every smile, every giggle, every word makes me want that girl more. The more time I spend with her, the more I picture fucking her all over the store.

So, I'm leaving Mat to handle her, to spend time with her.

I can't do it. I would rather him go crazy than me.

If I act on my urges, there will be nothing stopping me.

She's young; she should be enjoying her life, not getting fucked by a guy twelve years older than her.

But if I'm being honest, I would give her so much more pleasure than someone her age ever could. I would make her body sing with just the slightest touch.

"Another drink, Samuel?" Barry, the owner of Hometown Bar, asks.

"That would be great, Barry. Thanks." Maybe drinking will help me rid my head of thoughts of a certain girl.

"Coming right up." Within a minute, I have a fresh beer in front of me, and I try to chug my fantasies away.

"I see Booked got a new employee," Barry says. Small talk.

When I first threw out the idea of moving here and opening up a bookstore to my brother, I pitched it as a way for us to escape the lives our parents had lined up for us.

I think that's why I suggested we move to Crystal Springs —I didn't want to deal with all the shit that came with living as the son of a New York Socialite. That wasn't who I was.

So, I ran, and I brought my brother with me. Thankfully, he didn't put up a fight.

We had spent the first few years of our lives here, and when I was thinking of places we could escape to that weren't overly quiet or a far drive from a city if needed, we picked here. We had roots here, so it made it sense.

Reading had been my escape when I was a kid, and Crystal Lake became my escape when I got to my twenties. Booked seemed like a book name for the store, and it was a play on words, and thankfully my brother agreed so that's what we name it.

I take another swig of my beer before I answer Barry.

"Yeah, there's a new girl in town. Thought we could help her out a bit while she was here," I say to him.

The town is going to talk—they're all fucking chismosos—might as well tell him the fucking truth. If I don't, I'm sure a lie will soon circulate and make our lives a living hell.

"I'm glad you and Mat opened your doors for her. She looks young, and she definitely seemed scared when she arrived." I guess I wasn't the only one who noticed her when she stepped off the bus. "It will be good for her to have you two to help her get adjusted," Barry says with a bright smile, and all I can do is nod.

Yup. Though the two of us want to do a lot more to Zoey than take her under our wing.

Barry is called to the other side of the bar before I can come up with something to respond with. Thank fuck.

I'm finishing up my second beer when I hear the bell over the door chime, and not a minute later, the stool next to me is getting pulled out.

There is no need for me to turn to know my brother has arrived. He's the only one stupid enough to sit next to me. The townsfolk know not to ever bother me when I'm drinking. Well, besides Barry of course.

"You're an asshole, you know that?" he grumbles as he tries to get Barry's attention.

"Why am I an asshole this time?" I say, leveling him a look. I know why; I just want to see if he has the balls to say it out loud.

"You know why. You hired the girl, and now you're leaving me to spend all day with her," he whispers, as if he doesn't want anyone to hear him. "It's fucking torture. I'm going to have permanent blue balls because of you, and I'm stupid for going along with it," he grumbles.

"And you don't think it's torture for me? Every time I walk in there, I have to hold myself back from touching her."

Barry finally comes to hand us both fresh beers. We both take drinks, and when Barry is out of hearing distance, Mat speaks.

"We need to find a way to get her out of our heads. She's our employee; we can't be thinking about her like this. We have to respect her, and we have to do that by not constantly thinking about fucking her."

He's right. Of course, the fucker is always right.

"How do you suggest we get her out of our heads?" I'm open for any suggestions he might have.

He thinks about it for a second before he shakes his head. "I was going to say find someone to fuck and maybe that will help, but that's just childish. We aren't little boys anymore. We can't use women to get another out of our heads."

"Wow. Not something the Matias from then years ago would have said." I smirk at him, but I have to agree.

"The Matias from ten years ago only wanted pussy," he answers before taking a drink.

"And what do you want now?" We've talked somewhat of what we want out of our relationships, but up until now, we haven't had any that make us think about the long haul.

We're thirty-three—we've been in relationships, but nothing that got serious enough for us to move to the next step. Hell, the women we've dated here are either our friends or have since moved.

"It would be nice to have someone to come home to—other than your surly face."

I should punch him for that, but I get it. Coming home to someone who isn't my brother would definitely be nice.

"I'm with you on that," I say, and he just nods.

We both go silent, just taking in the noise of the bar.

I know what he might be thinking, because I'm thinking the same thing. Can Zoey be *that* person?

If she is, who will she be that person for?

Me or him?

We have shared women before, but it's never been anything outside of the bedroom.

We both want to be with her, but how will one brother be affected when she chooses the other?

I shake those thoughts from my head. I don't even know if she wants anything to do with either of us, and I'm over here throwing out assumptions like something is going to happen.

Zoey is twenty-one years old. She's probably not looking for anything serious, and if she is, maybe she only wants guys her own age. I doubt she wants someone closer to forty.

"Did you close the store?" I say, changing the subject, not wanting to think about my employee much longer. It's almost closing time, so he might have decided to call it an early day.

"No, Zoey is still there. I just needed to escape for a few minutes. I'm going to go back and close up."

I nod and finish my drink. "I'll go with you."

Am I using closing as an excuse to see Zoey? Yes, I fucking am. I'm a sadistic son of a bitch who likes to be tortured by something I can't have.

Mat nods, finishing up his own beer.

Within minutes, we're walking over to the bookstore.

A few steps, and I'll have eyes on Zoey. In a few steps, my day will be brighter.

CHAPTER 6

I never knew books could hold worlds upon worlds for someone to escape into, that there would be so many stories to captivate you. I'm going to have to thank Samuel and Matias for giving me the opportunity to discover how big the world can actually be.

We're near closing, and I know for a fact no customers are going to come in right now; plus, Matias left about half an hour ago. So, I grab the book Matias told me to try, and I head to the back of the store, to my favorite chair.

As soon as I'm settled, I start reading.

From the words on the back cover, I know it's a hockey romance where the athlete meets a nerdy girl. It sounds interesting enough.

The story starts well—boy meets girl, girl is nerdy and not someone the boy usually goes for. Boy tries his hardest to get the girl's attention, to show her he's not just an athlete.

I breeze through the first few chapters and make it to their first date. The book is filled with sweet and swoon-worthy moments, and when they kiss at the end of the night, I sigh happily.

I love this book already; still, I can't help but wonder what made Matias gravitate toward a book like this. It seems like it would be out of the norm for him. I get to the part when the couple heads back to his place. The kissing continues, but now clothes are coming off, and a lot of touching is happening.

Cunt.

Cock.

Tight.

Pound.

Fuck.

My eyes go wide with every new word. It's not like I didn't know those words existed, but my mom always said they were frowned upon and never should be said out loud or even thought of.

But I can't help but agree with Matias—the explicit scenes are beautifully written.

Word after word, paragraph after paragraph, I'm sucked in. I want to continue reading about how this couple explores each other's bodies.

As I read, this feeling deep inside me gets stronger and more uncomfortable—this feeling I've only had while around Matias and Samuel. When I wanted to feel their hands on my body. Have their lips against mine.

I felt that feeling in my core, right between my legs.

I'm feeling the same way now.

As I continue reading, the feeling only grows. When the

male character slides his tongue down his heroine's body, I feel like he's doing it to me. When I read the words *he takes her clit between his teeth*, I'm panting, wanting to relieve the discomfort.

The words continue to flow, and I find my hand is moving down my own body, to my chest, touching my nipples through my clothing.

I may be twenty-one, but this is the first time I've touched my body like this, and I like it.

My hand moves down my body as I continue to read. When the hero slides his cock into the heroine's pussy, my hand makes it to my own core. I rub myself through my leggings, trying to relieve some of the pressure building in me.

God. The feeling of my fingers is like nothing I've ever felt.

What I would give to feel Samuel or Matias' hands on me like this. I bet they would make me feel things no one else would ever be able to, like my own touch isn't able to do.

They look like the kind of men who know how to treat a woman's body right.

Forgetting about the book completely, I'm picturing the hero being replaced by Samuel and Matias.

I picture them in front of me, playing with me, showing just how they would help me relieve the pressure.

My hand slides under my leggings, because rubbing myself over them isn't doing it for me. I need more pressure.

I need more in general.

When my fingers meet my sensitive area, I let out a moan.

"Oh, fucking hell," a voice says. A voice that isn't mine. A voice that's masculine, one I know well.

I open my eyes, and I see that a few feet in front of me

stand the two individuals who were just flooding my fantasies.

A blush creeps up my face as I think about what I was just caught doing by my bosses.

As I wait for the two of them to say something, I can't help but wish that the ground would swallow me whole.

CHAPTER 7

Matias

This girl keeps on surprising me—first, when she walked into the bookstore almost a month ago, and now, as she sits in front of us, touching herself.

Samuel and I walked into the bookstore about a minute ago. It was quiet, so we thought maybe Zoey was in the stock room, getting ready to close.

We were dead wrong.

She wasn't in the stock room, but in the chair she claimed as hers, and what she was doing had us stopping in our tracks.

I thought maybe my mind was playing tricks on me. Maybe I wasn't seeing Zoey pleasuring herself, with her hand down her leggings as she moaned.

But my mind wasn't playing tricks, because when I spoke, her eyes went wide, her face red with embarrassment.

"What are you doing, cariño?" Sam asks.

Zoey scrambles to straighten, her hand sliding out to close the book she was reading.

"Just doing some reading," she says, her voice raspy and breathy. She tries to give us a smile, but it's a little off.

"Were you reading anything interesting?" I ask, crossing my arms and giving her a smirk. God, I want to grab her hand and put her fingers in my mouth so I can get a taste of her.

"Umm," she says, a little flustered, "just the book you suggested."

The book I suggested.

I don't know why, but knowing she was reading something I suggested turns me on.

Knowing that book, I can only guess the part she was reading.

Hoping she doesn't punch me, I approach her.

"And how are you liking it?" I say, kneeling so I'm at eye level with her, one of my hands landing on her thigh.

"I think it's one of my new favorite books," she whispers, her eyes looking everywhere but me.

"And why has it become one of your favorites?" Samuel asks, getting closer.

Zoey looks up at my brother, and her blush creeps up even more. "I-I was loving the story so far, and their chemistry," she breathes out.

Samuel crouches next to me, his hand landing on her other thigh.

It's as if this woman is our queen, and she has us at her mercy.

"Was that all you were loving?" I ask.

As we wait for her to speak, I rub little circles along her thigh, watching her close her eyes. Either she's enjoying our hands on her, or she's about to push us off, call us perverts, quit, and run to the police station.

"No," she breathes out, taking another deep breath. "I was enjoying the sex scene."

Hearing her say the word makes my cock grow a little harder in my jeans.

"Did you like reading about how he was touching her?" Samuel asks. Like me, he has read the book. He knows what happens and how steamy it can be.

As he asks, my hand moves up her leg, almost to her center. When I press my fingers along her inner thigh, Zoey lets out a moan. Her eyes are still closed, though, so there is no way to tell if they are filled with lust.

"Yes," she sighs.

"Is that why you were touching yourself? Because you liked what he was doing to her?" I ask, continuing to rub circles closer and closer to her covered pussy.

"Yes."

"Did you like touching yourself out here, in the open? Where anyone could walk in?" Samuel asks, and from the way he's talking, I know the bastard is just as affected by this as I am.

"I wasn't paying attention. I didn't care." She lets out a moan when my fingers finally press against her pussy. I can feel her heat and wetness seeping through the fabric.

"What were you thinking about while you were touching yourself, cariño?" I watch as Samuel moves his hand up her body to cup her left tit, playing with her nipple through her shirt.

"Both," she lets out.

One of us lets out a growl, though if I'm being honest, it could have been both of us.

"Who were you thinking about?" My fingers press against her pussy; I could easily make a hole in her leggings just to slide my finger inside her.

Zoey swallows, not saying a word. She finally opens her eyes to look at the both of us. Her eyes are filled with lust, want, need. She doesn't have to say the words to tell us who she was thinking about. We already know the answer.

"The two of you." Her breath hitches just at bit.

Even though we already knew, Sam and I let out a groan before we get back to the task at hand.

"What were you thinking?" Samuel starts to ask. "Were you thinking of us touching you like this?" I slide my finger against her covered core while Sam squeezes her breast. "Of us touching your pussy and your tits, marking them as ours?" We pause while Zoey lets out a moan. "Were you thinking of our mouths on you?" Mine salivates at the thought. "Our hands?"

"Yes," she lets out, her voice filled with pleasure.

I stand and tip her chin up so I can look into her eyes.

"Do you want us to touch you like you were imagining? Do we have your permission?"" No pause. No hesitation.

"Yes."

At the word leaving her mouth, we pounce. I press my lips against hers, and as soon as I get a taste of her, my head spins. She tastes amazing, and I never want to pull away.

I slide my tongue along her bottom lip, and she opens up for me. She lets out a little groan when my tongue meets hers —*fuck*, this girl is going to be the death of me.

I hear shifting, and when I pull back, I see Sam on his knees in front of her, dragging her leggings off.

"Are you going to show him how sweet your pussy is?" I run my thumb along her lower lip, her eyes widening, but not with fear—with wonder.

She nods but we need to hear her words.

"Speak, tesoro. We need to hear you say the word."

"Yes."

"Pruébala, hermano. Eat her pussy and tell me how good she tastes," I command.

"With fucking pleasure," Sam growls, and I know when his lips land on her, because Zoey's eyes roll back in ecstasy.

As Sam licks up every inch of her pussy, Zoey lets out the most delicious sounds I have ever heard. She looks like she wants to combust.

"Do you like that, tesoro? Do you like the way he fucks that pussy with his tongue?" She nods a yes to my questions. Not being able to help myself, I grab her chin and force her eyes to meet mine. "Say the words. Let us hear you say how much you like it."

"I love it," she says, her voice a seductive purr.

Another moan leaves her. Needing some form of relief, I grab the hand closest to me and place it on my bulging cock as she grinds her pussy against Samuel's face.

"Such a sweet cunt," Samuel groans out. My mouth waters at the thought of tasting her like he is.

"Finger her," I command. "Make our sweet girl come."

I tighten my grip on Zoey's hand and start moving it up and down my shaft for some friction as I watch Samuel insert a finger into her pussy, then two.

"She's fucking tight," he groans as he draws circles around her clit with his tongue.

"Do you like what he's doing to you, tesoro?" I say, pressing my lips to hers before she can say anything, swallowing yet another moan.

"Yes," she pants when I pull away from her. Her fingers tighten around my cock, and if it wasn't for the fact that I'm still wearing jeans, I'm sure it would be in her mouth.

She's close; I can tell by the way Samuel is groaning. I slide my hand down to her chest and push down her shirt until her breasts are exposed, taking one of her nipples into my mouth.

Within seconds, she's exploding all over Sam's face.

"That's it, cariño. Come all over my face. Let me taste you," Sam says, and Zoey trembles.

I move my mouth up back to hers, and our tongues dance as she comes down. When she is finally sated, Samuel takes my place, kissing her, letting her taste herself.

When he pulls back, he takes her chin and looks her straight in the eyes.

"Was that the first time someone has touched you like that?" he asks her.

I don't know how it's possible, but Zoey turns even redder. She looks up at him for a long, silent minute, and then she nods.

Fuck.

"You're a virgin?" I find myself asking out loud.

Again, she nods. This time, her face is filled with shame and embarrassment, the euphoria from a minute ago gone.

"Say the words, cariño," Samuel requests.

Zoey swallows. "Yes, I'm a virgin."

I lean forward and take her chin from Samuel, making her

look up at me, "You have nothing to be embarrassed about. That isn't what defines you."

Zoey stares up at me and nods, agreeing with my words. Still, I think she needs time to digest the words. She mostly likely thinks we're mad at her for not telling us, but she'd be wrong.

"Let's get you dressed so we can head up to the cabin," Sam suggests. That statement gets her attention, and she turns to him in surprise.

"Cabin?" she asks, as if for clarification.

"Yes, the cabin. Did you really think we were going to leave you after what we just did? We aren't fuckboys. We treat our women with respect, and we will do so as long as you let us. That is, if you want."

Zoey looks up at the both of us as we stand in front of her, like she's trying to figure out what to do.

For a second, I think she's going to tell us she just wants to go home and pretend this night never happened. If she said that, we would respect it and give her space.

But when she speaks, she takes us both by surprise.

"I want to." The three words come out with a curt nod, as if she has made up her mind and we can't change it.

Zoey gets dressed, and once we are all situated and the store is closed, we get into my truck, and the three of us drive up to the cabin.

I have a feeling there is no going back.

CHAPTER 8

SAMUEL

Her taste is still on my tongue, and it is fucking *delicious*.

When we walked into the bookstore and saw Zoey pleasuring herself, my mind imagined scenarios of what might come from the situation.

She would be embarrassed, quit, and walk away forever.

She would tell us she was sorry, leave, and then come back the next day as if nothing happened.

Never did I think she would let us touch her. Never did I think that she would let me tongue fuck her or even finger fuck her until she came.

But she did, and the sight of it will be forever embedded in my mind.

Zoey looked beautiful riding my face, with her eyes rolled back in pleasure and her back arching, pleading for attention.

When I slipped my fingers into her and felt how tight she

was, that's when I knew no one had touched her this way. That thought alone made me want more of her. There was something primal about being her first. Even half an hour later, I'm still marveling at the fact that I was the first man who has had the pleasure to taste her.

I suggested we all go to the cabin, because I couldn't leave her. I wanted her in my arms, wanted my touch on her somehow. Thankfully, she agreed.

Now, we're in Matias' truck heading up to our cabin, Zoey sitting between the two of us, one of our hands on each of her thighs.

I didn't think she'd let us touch her after the bookstore, but I was wrong.

This girl keeps on surprising me.

Matias pulls the truck into the triple garage, one of the benefits of living and owning so much land—you can build your house however you want.

"This is where you live?" Zoey asks, marveling at the house through the windshield.

"We do. Come—we will give you a tour," Matias says to her when the truck is parked and he is out of the cab. He holds his hand out for her, and she slides out after him.

While Matias shows Zoey the house, I start up dinner. If this night is going to go the way I think it is, we are going to need sustenance. Even if it doesn't go in that direction, eating is still a good idea.

When dinner is almost ready, Matias and Zoey finally reappear in the kitchen, Zoey with bright smile on her face that brings out one of my own.

"You two have a beautiful home. It makes my apartment look like a box," she says brightly.

"I doubt your place is that small," I say, making a plate for her.

"It is, but I like it," she answers, rewarding me with another beautiful smile.

No doubt in my mind, this woman is going to pull every smile I've been holding in for God knows how long.

With a smile thrown in her direction, I hand her a dinner plate. "Dinner is served."

It doesn't take long for the three of us to get settled at the kitchen island. Not being able to help myself, I maneuver us so Zoey is between Matias and me.

Once we're all settled, we eat dinner in silence. When it's just me and Matias, I'm okay with silence, but now that Zoey is here, it feels slightly awkward.

"So, Zoey, how are you liking working at Booked?" I say awkwardly.

Fuck. I hate small talk.

I hear Matias snort at my attempt to start a conversation.

Thankfully, Zoey notices and answers. "I like it, and that's not me just trying to suck up. You two have an amazing selection, and I can see why you're successful. It also doesn't hurt that you're amazing bosses and make it easy to want to get out of bed in the morning. I look forward to walking into the bookstore every day."

A blush creeps up my cheeks as she says the words. Given what happened earlier, she likes more than just working there. At least, I hope she does.

"Well, I'm glad you like it," I say, and I cringe at how that sounds.

"Thank you for giving me the opportunity." She flashes me

a sweet smile, and I wish I could lean over and kiss her just for the hell of it.

Matias clears his throat, and our attention goes to him.

"I really enjoy small talk as much as the next guy, but I think it would be wise to talk about what happened at the store. We can't just avoid it."

A sigh escapes me.

My brother is right.

We can't act like it didn't happen. It did, and fuck, I really hope it happens again.

Even if it's a year from now, I hope it happens again.

"He's right. We really do need to talk about what happened," I say to Zoey, who is looking down at her plate.

I look at my brother, and he looks back at me. We know we have to tread lightly here and leave everything in her court. She has to be the one who makes the decisions, not us. She's the ruler, and we are waiting for her command. Whatever it may be, we will follow.

We sit in silence for a few minutes before Zoey works up the courage to break it.

"Is it wrong for me to say I want it to happen again?" she asks, her voice almost a whisper, as if she's afraid of telling us the truth.

"No, it's not wrong," Mat says to her, brushing her hair from her shoulder.

"Would it also be wrong for me to want the two of you at the same time? I don't want to choose one or the other." Zoey finally turns to look at me and then looks to Matias.

"No, there would be nothing wrong with that either," I tell her.

And it's the truth. There is nothing wrong with her

choosing the both of us. As long as we are all okay with it, that is all that matters.

She nods. "What would this be, though? Would it just be a sexual thing? Will it be more?" Her face grows more concerned with each question.

They are valid questions, definitely things she should have the answers to.

"How about we move this conversation to the living room?" I suggest, wanting to be more comfortable and thankfully, they both nod.

We head into the living room and get situated, Zoey on the couch and Matias and I sitting on the coffee table in front of her.

"I think the first question we should tackle is what do you want this to be?" I ask her.

She bites her bottom lip and contemplates the question. Her eyes bounce between the two of us, as if she is trying to decide.

"I want..." She pauses but then quickly continues. "I want to be with both of you. I don't want to choose."

Her words have a strength behind them, as if that's the one thing she is sure about.

"Tesoro, you can have us both. You don't have to choose," Matias tells her.

If she felt like she did have to choose, I think I would walk away. I've shared plenty of women with my brother, but if she didn't want me as I wanted her and I had to see the two of them be happy, I don't think I would be able to do it. I would let Matias have her whole heartedly and walk away so I wouldn't break watching it.

Thankfully, that doesn't look like it's going to happen.

She goes silent as she contemplates what she is going to say next. "How would it work? I mean, I have an idea how the, um, sex would go, but what about the rest of it?"

"Do you want this to be more than just sex?" I ask her.

"I think I do," she answers. "I don't have a whole lot of experience, but I don't know if I would be able to have sex and walk away. Knowing myself, feelings will be involved, and I won't be able to separate the two. But what I want may not be necessarily what you two want."

Her eyes move back to her hands.

Not being able to help myself, I lean over just enough to grab her left hand in mine.

"Zoey, for the last month, we both have been fighting with ourselves over wanting to be with you. If you wanted to try a relationship, I'm pretty sure we would give it to you. If you simply wanted sex, we would give that to you too. This ball is in your court," I say, giving her hand a tight squeeze.

She finally looks up. "You both want to be with me?" She asks like it's the most ridiculous thing in the world.

"Yes, we do," I answer. When the words leave my mouth, she gives a bright smile, like she can't believe it.

Honestly, I can't either. I for sure thought we would keep that piece of information to ourselves until she was long gone from Crystal Springs.

Matias gets up from his place on the coffee table and goes to sit next to her on the couch. I watch as he takes her other hand and brings it to his lips, placing a kiss against her knuckles.

"Whatever you want, we will give you. You just have to make the decision. We won't make it for you. We won't force whatever this is. You make the rules, not us," Matias tells her, giving each one of her knuckles a kiss.

"What will the people in town say?" she asks, turning to me for an answer.

I let out a growl. "Fuck them. As long as you're happy with whatever decision you make, it doesn't matter what anyone else thinks."

Sure, the townsfolk will talk, but I don't give a rat's ass. If this is going to happen and Zoey is going to be our girl, then we will protect her in any way we can, crazy ass rumors included.

"It will just be us three. No one else will matter," Matias reassures her.

"Is that something you two would want? A relationship? With someone as young as me?" she asks, looking between the two of us.

I take my brother's lead and sit on her other side. Her hand never leaves mine.

"Age is just a number, right? You being twenty-one and inexperienced doesn't matter to us, but the question is: do you want to be with two men in their thirties?"

"Absolutely," she says with a nod, but then she moves the conversation in a different direction. "Can I be honest?"

"Of course," Matias answers.

"You two are the only men who have ever made me feel something. I have never wanted to be with someone as much as I want to be with the two of you. So, I want to give it a try, see if we can become something other than sexual frustration making its way out. If you two are willing." Her eyes dance with her words.

I look at my brother above Zoey's head and silently ask

what he thinks. There is no reason to say the words out loud when I know what he thinks, because I think the same thing.

"We are willing," I say to the beautiful woman between my brother and me.

"You are?" She turns her head to us.

"We are," Matias answers.

Zoey's face transforms into a bright smile as her head swivels between the two of us.

"Ok, so what happens now?"

"Now, we seal the deal with a kiss."

CHAPTER 9

Zoey

*S*eal the deal with a kiss.

I'm still trying to figure out what that means when two sets of lips land on my skin. My head flies back in pleasure as these two men explore every inch of my neck.

"You taste so good, Tesoro," Matias says against my skin, goosebumps covering my whole body.

I feel hands on my body, pulling me in one direction and then another. My lower lip is trembling, wanting to feel a set of lips against them.

Samuel must hear my silent cry, because he abandons my neck and moves up until his lips are pressed against mine. His tongue slides against my bottom lip, and I open my mouth to let him in. A moan escapes me when I feel his tongue slide between my lips.

Never in my life have I been kissed like this. Never has a man dominated my mouth, my tongue, in the way Samuel is.

I've kissed boys before, but not a single kiss has ever felt like this one does. I never want it to end.

As Samuel devours my mouth, I feel Matias moving down my body. Somehow, I'm pushed so my back is against the couch cushion. My shirt rides up in the process, and I feel Matias' hands on my breast.

"You have wonderful tits, Tesoro. I just want to suck on them y marcarlas como mías." I moan at his words. I took enough Spanish to know he wants to make my breast as his.

I want to tell him to do it, to mark me, but I don't know how to form the words to scream.

Samuel grunts before he pulls back from me. I miss him when he's gone.

"I think we should both mark her; that, way the whole town knows who she belongs to." He looks into my eyes, a power in them I really like seeing.

Matias stands and looks at me and his brother. "Should we take this conversation upstairs?"

Samuel nods. "I think we should. What do you say, our beautiful Zoey? Should we go upstairs?"

Our.

He called me theirs.

I look up at them, and I know before I even say the words that my mind is already made up.

"Take me upstairs," I breathe.

Without as much as a warning, Matias bends down, picks me up, and throws me over his shoulder, making his way up to the second floor.

I laugh the whole way up, which earns me a slap on the butt—a slap that might have triggered a moan to leave my mouth.

Once on the second floor, Matias walks us down the hall and finally into a room. He wastes no time laying me in the middle of a bed—*his* bed.

I don't know what I expected. Maybe still the bedroom of a teenage boy, but never did I think it was going to be organized and clean, filled with blues and creams.

"I feel like you need to be naked. We need to see that glorious body of yours without anything covering it," Samuel says, walking over to the bed.

With one knee up on the mattress, he grabs me by the legs and drags me closer to him. When my butt meets the edge of the bed, his hands travel to the waistband of my leggings, and he pulls them off, quickly followed by my panties.

This is the second time tonight he has done this; I think I love it more every time.

"Mmm, such a pretty pussy," he says, licking his lips as he stares at my bare core.

Samuel runs a finger through my slit, feeling my wetness, and I shudder.

"Already wet. Do you like the thought of what we're about to do to you, cariño?"

God, his words. I love it when he calls me cariño, and I don't think I will ever grow tired of hearing it. Same for when Matias calls me tesoro.

I nod. "Yes."

I'm staring up at Samuel as he stands to full height, and I hear Matias shuffling around until I finally feel his hands back on my stomach.

"This needs to go," he grunts, lifting my shirt and pulling it over my head. When my shirt is on the floor, he takes a second to admire my chest covered in lace. He licks his lips before he undoes my bra.

I'm completely bare to them now.

They look down at my body, not saying a word. For a second, I feel all the confidence in me drain away. I'm sure they are used to women who are skinner than I am, who may have a flat stomach and not so wide hips.

I'm about to cover myself with my arms, but I stop when they start to move.

It's Samuel who has me throwing all insecurities out the window.

"Do not cover yourself up. We want to see every beautiful inch of you," he says as he comes to where my head rests while Matias widens my legs and stands between them.

"No sex tonight," Matias announces as he slides his finger along my slit, covering my pussy with my wetness.

I feel my eyes going wide. I think a part of me was preparing myself to have sex tonight. What else would you think when you are completely naked in front of two hot men?

"We are going to take it a little slow tonight, but just because you won't have one of our cocks in your pussy doesn't mean you won't have a good time." Samuel strokes my cheek and pushes my hair back.

"Do I get to see all of you too?" I ask. It's only fair.

"We'll give you anything you want, baby," Matias says, pulling his shirt off right way.

Samuel follows close behind, and once the shirts come off, so does the rest of their clothing.

When they are both fully naked, I cannot form words.

Their bodies are what you would imagine Greek gods' to

be. There is no way in hell these men are real, that they want me of all people.

Without thinking, I reach out to touch them. I need to feel them, to see for myself that they are real.

Their muscles flex the moment my fingers graze their stomachs. They really are twins, with the same reactions.

My eyes travel from their abs to what they have below the waist.

Oh my.

Big.

Big Cocks.

Really big cocks.

Fuck.

When we get to the sex part, are they going to fit inside me? They are both long and hard and thick.

My hands slide down their stomachs, and when I touch them both below the waist, they let out a simultaneous groan.

"Fuck," Samuel lets out, and the next thing I know, I'm on my back.

"You'll get to play in a little bit. It's our turn right now." I'm about to rebut Matias' statement, but I'm silenced when his mouth lands on my pussy. My eyes close, and I'm swarmed with pleasure.

"How good does she taste?" Samuel asks, getting situated by my head.

"Better than I ever fucking imagined," Matias says against my core, the words vibrating through my body.

I can barely control my breathing as his tongue slides up and down my slit and circles my clit.

"Do you like what he's doing, baby? Do you like when his

tongue plays with you?" Samuel asks, one of his hands landing on my chest, pulling and twisting my nipple.

I nod, and when I open my eyes, I'm face to face with Samuel's cock.

I want to lick it. To run my tongue all over it. To have him fill my mouth. I've never given a blow job before, but there's a first time for everything, and I want him to be my first.

Leaning forward, I get close enough to run my tongue along his tip and draw little circles on the head. Samuel lets out a grunt and what sounds like a growl when I take him fully into my mouth.

"Holy fuck." His hands go to my head to hold me steady as I work him, and Matias works me.

"Such a good slut," Samuel praises, his words making me wetter by the second. "You're working my cock so damn well, cariño. Makes me want to fuck your mouth."

I let out a moan and pull his cock out when I can't seem to catch my breath with what Matias is doing.

There is a feeling in my stomach that is getting tighter and tighter. It's a sensation I feel all the way to my toes.

"You taste so good. I could eat you every single day and not get tired of it." Matias comes up for air and gives my thigh a few nibbles before he goes back to my pussy. This time, he takes my clit between his lips and sucks, eating at me like I'm his favorite dessert while finger fucking me hard.

"So tight. I can't wait to feel you wrapped around my cock."

"More," I pant.

"Did you hear that, hermano? It sounds like our little slut wants more," Samuel says before he strokes my lower lip with his cock. My tongue pokes out, and I can taste the pre-cum leaking out of him.

"I think we should give her everything she wants." Matias slides his tongue through my folds again, but this time, he doesn't stop at my opening. He continues all the way to my back side, licking my puckered hole like he was my pussy.

Anal sex has never interested me before, and honestly, I have never looked at it as an option—until now.

"Oh my God," I practically scream when he continues to circle his tongue against my hole, making me wish he was doing more.

"She likes her ass played with," he muses and continues with his tongue until I feel a finger rubbing against me.

I let out a shiver that doesn't go unnoticed.

"Soon, cariño. Soon, you will be filled with both of us, and you won't know what to do but scream our names."

The dirty talk. I don't know how much I can take.

"Fuck her mouth," Matias tells Samuel as he makes his way back to my pussy to finger fuck me.

"Gladly." Samuel guides my head back to his cock, and I take as much as I can as he thrusts into my mouth. I feel him at the back of my throat as tears come down my face.

I feel Matias as he moves his fingers and tongue in and out of me so rapidly, I can't tell where anything starts or ends, my body tightening even more.

"That's it, tesoro. Come on my hand. Fuck my fingers with this greedy pussy." My legs shake at his words, and I feel myself explode around him, my wetness going everywhere.

"Fuck. Fuck!" I scream around Samuel.

"So hot. So sweet," Matias says, taking my release and coating himself with it, pumping up and down on his cock.

I keep my eyes on Matias as I swallow as much of Samuel as I can. I think he might be close; the only sign I have is how tight he's holding my head to his body.

"Milk my cock, cariño. Milk me until I fill that pretty mouth of yours with my cum." I place a hand on his balls, rubbing him as he groans.

Matias is watching us, and I can see it in his lust filled eyes: he's close.

"I'm going to come, baby," Samuel grunts before pulling out of my mouth and taking himself in his hand.

Both brothers situate themselves over me, stroking themselves, and before I know it, they cover my body in their cum.

When they finish, they each lean down and give me a kiss, and as they pull away, I run a finger along my chest, bringing their releases to my mouth.

I moan at the taste of the two of them on my tongue.

"Fuck. I think I'm ready for round two after seeing that," Matias groans, and all I do is smile at them.

We clean up the mess we just made, and after they go down to check everything is locked for the night, they both come back to bed and lay down with me.

I have Samuel at my back and Matias at my front, and I have never had a more peaceful sleep in my life.

Looks like I will be booked for the rest of winter.

Matias

I swear, I'm fucking dreaming.

No way in hell is what I'm experiencing right now actually happening. No way is a wet, hot mouth sliding up and down my cock, waking me from my slumber.

Sure enough, when I open my eyes, it's not a dream. A mouth really is sliding up and down my cock. Zoey's mouth, to be exact.

Her blonde hair is a mess, covering her face. My hand lifts involuntarily, moving her hair out of the way so I can see her take me.

She sucks on my tip, and I swear, I see fucking stars.

"Fuck. I love this wake up call," I say, enjoying what her mouth is doing to me. Turning my head, I notice my brother is also awake, watching our girl take my cock in her mouth, one of her hands wrapped around his cock. Zoey releases my cock with a pop and switches over to Samuel's, her hand coming to me.

"Fuck, she sure knows how to use that mouth," Samuel grunts, and I see Zoey smirk.

As she takes Samuel's cock deeper, her ass goes up in the air, just asking for attention.

Moving from under her hand, I go to the foot of the bed and lick my lips when I get a clear view of her round cheeks.

I run my hands along her smooth skin, gripping each globe, opening her—her pussy is already glistening wet.

"This pussy is asking to be fucked." I run my finger from her asshole to her clit and lean down, placing my mouth on her.

Fuck. She tastes so good. I think I will have her for breakfast, lunch, dinner, and every single snack in between.

"Then fuck it," Zoey lets out, lifting her head from Samuel's cock for a quick second to speak before taking it again.

"I will, baby. We have to work up to it," I say, giving her ass a smack.

Zoey yelps before pulling away from Sam and settling herself at the top of the bed, her back against the headboard and her legs wide for us to see. Looking between me and Samuel, she slowly slides her hand down her body, all the way to her pussy.

"It's going to happen. The time will come when both of you will fuck me. You both already had your tongues inside me; why wait any longer to fully claim me? I'm ready."

I watch as she circles her clit and then slides her finger to her entrance, slowly fucking herself.

Fuck. When did this girl get so damn confident? Wasn't she just hiding from us?

Have we corrupted her already?

"Cariño," Samuel lets out as his hand slowly caresses her leg.

"Fuck me," she says with determination. I think I like hearing her curse like that. In the time she has been here, that she has worked for us, she has been the perfect lady, not a swear word in sight.

I look at my brother, silently asking what we should do. He raises an eyebrow, and I can see it in his face: he wants her to do whatever she wants just as much as I do.

If Zoey wants this, then we would take our time with her, nothing too rough or hard.

I don't know if I've ever taken someone's virginity, so for some reason, this scenario is making me a little nervous—and I'm not a nervous person.

I give him a slight nod—if he is up for it, then I am too. We both want this girl, so let's officially make her ours.

Without a word, Samuel in his position, and I climb back on the bed, taking my place at Zoey's side as she watches every move.

Reaching up, I place a hand on her cheek, running feather-like strokes against her skin.

"We will take care of you. If you really want to do this, we will make sure you are okay and enjoying yourself," I say before placing a light kiss on her lips.

When I pull back, her eyes are filled with lust, asking for more.

"I want this," she whispers against my lips.

"Then let us give it to you," Samuel says, inching closer to her on the bed so he can place kiss after kiss down her body.

As he showers her with kisses, I press my lips against hers. She tastes as sweet as she did last night, and I get lost in *her*.

This girl has made her way into my head, and she is trying to make her way into my heart. I might just let her.

I can feel Zoey squirming under our touch, asking for more. Samuel must hear her silent cries, because the bed shifts, and he is situated between her legs, eating his first meal of the day.

"I'll give her the first orgasm, and you give the second." He's going to let me be the one to fuck her first. God, it's times like these I could tell the grumpy fucker I actually like him.

But, if we are both going to have her, this must be fair.

"We both fuck her."

He smirks before diving back into her deliciousness.

Zoey getting pleasured sure is a sight. I kiss her and play with her tits as Samuel tongue fucks her. I swallow every moan and groan she lets out.

"That's it, cariño. Fuck my face. Take what you want," Samuel growls, and Zoey pulls ways from me, her orgasm taking over her body.

As Zoey calms down, he kisses up her body before taking her mouth, giving her a taste of her release. When they pull apart, I lean forward and kiss her, getting a taste for myself. She's delicious on her tongue.

I move from her lips down her neck, to her chest, all the way to her pussy. I lick at her wetness, at her release, before straightening back up and situating myself between her legs.

Grabbing my cock, I slide it along her lips, coating myself

in her first orgasm, thinking how badly I want to slide into her and stay wrapped in her warmth for days.

"Condom," Samuel interrupts, and I instantly want to slap myself over the head.

Fuck, I was about to slide into her bare. It would have felt amazing, but it would have been stupid of me.

With a shake of my head, I go to my nightstand and grab a condom. Once I'm wrapped up, I retake my place between Zoey's thighs.

I coat my cock with her arousal again, but before I slide into her, I lean down to place her kisses along her stomach, her chest.

"Are you sure you want to do this?" The question comes out soft. "This happens, and there is no going back for us," I say, peppering kisses along her skin.

There is no hesitation in her voice. "Yes, I'm sure."

I lean back just enough to look into her eyes.

There's a bit of fear swimming in them, but the feeling is over powered by confidence, lust, and determination.

Fuck, I can give this girl everything, and it wouldn't be enough.

With one final nod, I guide my cock to her entrance and slowly press myself inside. My eyes move up to hers as I slide in, only to find that her eyes are closed tightly, as if she is preparing for all the pain. I try to comfort her, placing my hands against her thighs and giving them a reassuring squeeze.

"Breathe, tesoro. You need to remember to breathe."

She takes a deep breath, and I feel her relax a bit. When she takes another, I slide deeper.

I continue to guide myself in with her breaths until I'm

fully seated, and holy damn, she is so damn tight, it feels like she might cut off circulation to my cock.

It's fucking marvelous.

"Fuck, you're so damn tight," I groan, not wanting to move.

"Nice and slow," Sam says, and I look over to see him stroking Zoey's face, trying to make her as comfortable as possible. "Just relax, cariño. Just relax. Breathe."

Zoey lets out another breath, and after what may be a minute, she gives me a nod, as if giving me permission to move.

I don't just yet. Instead, I lean forward, wiping away the beads of sweat forming along her temples.

"Are you okay?" I ask, afraid I'm hurting her or that she doesn't like the feeling of me inside her. The look on her face tells me she might be in pain and that she's a second away from backing out.

But she nods, her eyes still very much closed. "Maybe if you move, it will be better," she pants.

"Don't fucking hurt her," Samuel growls. If I wasn't inside our girl right now, I would punch him for even thinking I would do such a thing. But then I remember how, if he was in my position, I would be making the same command.

With another nod of confirmation from my beautiful girl, I start to move, my hands pressing into her hips, trying to control myself from doing something that may hurt Zoey in any way.

I continue to move at a slow pace until Zoey becomes impatient.

"More," she pants.

"I don't want to hurt you," I tell her, trying to control my breathing.

"You won't. Please. Move faster," she begs.

Before I do anything, I look over at my brother, as if to ask if I should follow her orders, and all he does is nod. If our girl wants more, we are going to fucking giver her more.

With a grunt, I start to thrust faster and harder until Zoey's moans get louder, and I feel her tighten around me. I press my fingers harder into her skin, and she lets out another moan.

I don't know how long I'm inside her, but after a few thrusts, her pussy starts to tighten even more. When Samuel reaches over and rubs her clit, she explodes around me, milking my cock for everything I have. It's her second orgasm of the morning, shaking through her body in a way she probably didn't expect.

"Fuck," I grunt, pulling out of her and rolling off the condom, painting Zoey with my release. I take note of the small streaks of blood that coat it. She just gave me her virginity, and for some reason, knowing that has something primal brewing inside me. It only intensifies my orgasm all over my girl's stomach.

It was so damn intense that I start seeing black spots and my breathing hard. Not having any energy whatsoever, I fall to Zoey's side, where she has relaxed against my mattress. When I look over at her, she looks just as spent as I feel.

But her breathing becomes more labored, Sam kissing her neck and playing with her tits, trying to bring her down from the high.

Never have I seen my brother so caring. Usually when we fuck women together, he doesn't caress them like this, doesn't cuddle. He just fucks them and fucks them some more. This side of him is different.

I guess it takes a woman like Zoey to change him.

Under his touch, Zoey shifts to face him, and even though I can't see her, I'm sure she's giving him a sleepy smile.

"Your turn," she whispers, and I hear Sam chuckle.

"I'll take my turn, but not right now. Let your body rest. I'll get my turn later," he tells her, planting a kiss on her lips.

Zoey must be content with his answer, because she sighs and cuddles deeper into the bed, wrapping her arms around Sam and tangling her legs with mine.

If every morning starts like this, I will be a happy man.

Without a fucking doubt.

CHAPTER 11

SAMUEL

*I*t didn't take a lot of convincing, but Zoey is officially ours, and no one can take that away from us.

Mat claimed her three weeks ago, and then a few hours later, it was my turn. I knew she would be sore, so I tried to be as gentle with her as I could. Keyword—tried.

Gentle went out the door once she started telling me to go harder and faster and that she didn't care if she couldn't walk afterwards.

I wanted to keep her happy, so I gave her what she wanted. It was hard and it was fast, but when her pussy tightened around my cock, I saw fucking stairs.

I will be dreaming about her cunt for years to come.

That day and the ones after it felt nice, particularly to have someone else in the house besides my brother. It's been good to hearing her laugh and her voice throughout my day, not only at work. It has been soothing.

These last three weeks have been a whirlwind—a lot of sex, sleepovers, and everything in between.

It's been better than I ever thought it could be.

This morning, before coming to the store, I dropped off Zoey at her apartment so she could have some time for herself and get ready for the workday.

We've talked about being at the house for more than just a handful of hours, but she's not there just yet. This is all moving way to quickly, and we want to give her all the time she needs before we go changing her life again with something like a move.

She came in to the store about an hour ago, and now, we're trying to work while sneaking in a few make out sessions here and there. That's how work has been going these last few weeks: make out session after make out session. I'm not ashamed to say we have christened about sixty percent of the store.

Matias and I can't seem to keep our hands to ourselves when she is around, which and as soon as the store closes, it's as if we have to ravish her and cannot wait until we make it home. Since our busy season starts in a few days and more staff will start coming in, we need to learn how to control ourselves within the walls of the store.

"I'm heading to Sacramento for the meeting," Matias announces a little bit after lunch.

Going to Sacramento is a monthly thing for us. We alternate who makes the drive down to the Central Valley, and this month is his turn. Usually, it's for meetings or conventions with other booksellers. This time, we've been having issues with some of the books we've been receiving from a small press in the area, so Mat is going to meet with the printer and distributor to see what can be done.

"Sounds good," I say with nod. Zoey must have heard, because she comes out of the stock room and goes straight for him.

"I'll be back tonight," he tells her before giving her a kiss on the lips and heading out the door.

It's interesting how in three weeks' time, everything changed. There are no complaints on my part; it just blows my mind at how quick things moved.

Nearly a month ago, she was just an employee, someone Mat and I wanted to fuck. Now, she has become so much more.

Once Mat is gone, Zoey wraps her arms around my neck, her lips against mine.

"How are you feeling?" I ask, placing a kiss just under her ear.

"A little sore, but nothing I can't handle," she purrs.

"That's good," I mutter into her skin; I nibble just below her pulse point before I pull back. "What do you feel like having for dinner?" I ask as my hands go straight to her ass and bring her closer to my body.

"Does having you for dinner count?" She gives me a sly grin as I growl.

"How about we let you rest tonight, and we go back to this topic tomorrow?" I kiss the tip of her nose, trying to sweeten her up.

We've been going at it multiple times a day for three weeks —that's a lot on one's body. She says she doesn't care about the discomfort or soreness, but I do. I don't want to hurt her, so we will take a break if necessary.

Zoey nods. "Okay."

When the bookstore is closed for the day and all locked up, Zoey and I decide to head to the bar to have dinner. It didn't seem like a bad idea to me, but then I remembered that Zoey, even though she's of age, she doesn't drink. She just has no desire to, she said.

When I suggested we go somewhere else, she shook her head. "It's fine. I'll have iced tea. I can enjoy my time with you anywhere." She gives me a chaste kiss before she heads to a table in the back.

All I do is smile as I make my way to join her. Our interaction caught the eye of a few townsfolk, but nobody has the balls to say anything about it to my face.

Once we settle into the table and place our order, I turn to Zoey, who's smiling bright.

"So, I never asked. Why Crystal Springs?" I ask, leaning closer to her.

She sighs. "I don't know. It seemed like a good idea at the time. When I finally decided to leave home, I looked for small towns in California and found this place. All the pictures I saw were the most beautiful landscapes, and it looked like a good place to escape to. Now, here I am."

"Where is home?" I ask, taking one of her hands .

"West Virginia. I lived there with my mom," she states.

"And was she happy with you moving across the country?" I'm trying to get to know her better. I don't want our relationship to be just about sex.

She makes a face that tells me her mother was, in fact, not happy that she left home.

"She had a hard time accepting I wanted to grow into my own person. As far as I know, she wanted to keep me at home for as long as possible. But I needed to get out. I needed to forge my own path, not the one she had set for me."

I guess we have that in common. We both had paths set for us by our parents, and we abandoned them.

"I know that all too well," I say to her.

"You do?" Her eyes go wide with surprise.

I nod, "Yeah, our parents are what you would call influential. Our whole lives, they have had everything planned out—what schools we would go to, where we would live, what we were going to wear. Everything. After a while, it started to take a toll, so when we graduated college, I suggested to Matias we move here after coming into our own money and wealth, and he agreed. Now, here we are."

"I guess we have that in common, but I bet your parents were not overbearing like Mother is." Her eyebrows bunch up, and all I want to do is smooth them out.

"I don't know, our parents were pretty bad. I doubt they would compare to yours." I try to say it in a joking manner, and it partly works, but I don't get the smile I was hoping for.

"Well, you weren't raised by a former cult member. I was raised to believe that ninety percent of what happens in the world is evil and goes against a book that wants to be the Bible but isn't. Everything had to do with what was good in the eyes of that book—the music I listened to, the type of movies I watched, even the books I could have read. It all had to be tied back to whatever my mom was taught by a bunch of crazy people."

Fuck.

I completely forgot there are people in this world who live

that way. There is nothing against it, but it seems like it might have been forced upon Zoey instead of something she chose for herself.

"Is that why you left West Virginia? You wanted to escape that?"

"I wouldn't say escape. It was more along the line of I wanted to see what was out there. I wanted to see the world for myself, see if everything I'd been told was true. I didn't throw whatever faith I had in my mom's system away, I just wanted to broaden it."

I nod, completely understanding what she's saying. I was there once, where she is now, and I'm glad she went out to find what she wanted.

If she hadn't, she wouldn't have walked into our bookstore, and Matias and I wouldn't have her in our lives.

"Well, I'm glad you took that escape. Otherwise, you wouldn't be here with us." I lean over the small table between us and place a kiss on her lips.

The second our lips touch, I grow hungry for this girl. I want to feel her body squirm under mine. I want to have the taste of her pussy, sweet and tangy, on my tongue.

A throat clears somewhere close by, and if I hadn't heard it, I might have finger fucked Zoey right here, for everyone to see.

We pull back, and the waitress places our food in front of us before she scurries away. I can't help but laugh.

For the rest of dinner, Zoey and I get to know each other more.

She asks what it was like to have a twin growing up, and I ask her more about her life back home.

It's fascinating hearing her talk about her other life, as if she is a completely different person than the one I have come to know in the two months.

Once dinner is done and paid for, I take her hand, and we head out to the town square and enjoy the luminous night that, at times, feels like we can only experience in the Sierras.

"Can I ask you something?" she asks as we walk by the hardware store.

"You can ask anything you want."

She contemplates my words, sucking her bottom lip between her teeth. It takes her a second, but she finally speaks.

"Have there been others?" she asks, looking around. "Other women you and Matias have shared?"

Well, that wasn't what I thought she would ask. I understand the curiosity, but still, I'm caught off guard.

"Um…" I start to say, not really knowing how to go about this conversation.

"You know what, I don't need to know," she says, starting to walk away from me.

Grabbing her hand, I pull her back and grab her chin so she looks at me when I speak to her.

"Yes, there have been other women my brother and I have shared." I might as well be truthful with her. "But not in this capacity. We have shared women sexually, but never like this, never like what we're doing with you. You are different. This," I point between her and me, "is different."

Zoey is the type of person who shows her emotions through her eyes. I see her digesting my words, trying to figure out if they're true.

They are.

She is different from any other woman we have ever been with.

"Okay," she says, nodding, accepting my answer.

"Okay." I place a kiss on the tip of her nose and throw an arm around her shoulders.

We walk in silence back to the bookstore, and when we pass the bus station, she stops dead in her tracks.

"Zoey, you okay?" Her eyes are wide, and all the color from her face has drained, almost like she's seen a ghost. I look around trying to find something or someone who might have spooked her, but there are only people getting off a bus.

"Cariño, what's wrong?" I wrap an arm around her waist, bringing her closer, protecting her from the unknown.

She doesn't say anything; she just maintains a blank stare at the bus stop.

"Zoey Marie Thomas!"

Her full name rings out, and all I can think is...what the hell?

ZOEY

One second, I'm cuddling into Samuel's side, enjoying the life I chose for myself, and the next, I'm staring right into my mother's eyes.

How did she find me?

How the hell did she know where I am?

How is she even here?

I swear, I didn't leave any strings behind that might lead her to me. I got a new phone and a new number, and I've been using cash instead of credit cards. The only thing I could think of is that I used my real name for my rental and for the paperwork Booked. But would she seriously have someone run my social security number just to find me?

My mother has no boundaries, so I think she would.

"Zoey Marie Thomas!" she yells out, like she doesn't have my attention already.

"Who is that?" I hear Samuel ask, but I can't seem to form the words to tell him it's my mother.

All I can do is stand there like a statue and take in her anger-filled face.

"You have some nerve, young lady. I cannot believe you would do this, especially to your own mother," she yells as she gets closer to me, and when she's mere inches from us, she pulls at my arm, dragging me to her.

"Don't touch her," Samuel growls, and right away, my mother drops my arm, staring at the man next to me in shock.

"Who are you?" my mother asks him, angry he spoke to her in that manner.

"Her boyfriend. Who the fuck are you?" Samuel says through clenched teeth.

Any other time, I would be marveling at the fact that he called himself my boyfriend, but not right now. Not with my mother fuming in front of me.

"Her mother. And boyfriend? You look older, which would make any type of relationship with my daughter inappropriate," she spits at him.

Inappropriate in her eyes. She can't keep me as a twelve-year-old girl forever.

"Her mother?" Samuel asks, looking at back me with wide eyes. I close my eyes, hoping it will all end, but I nod to him that she is, indeed, my mother.

Taking a few deep breaths, I try to center myself before speaking. "What are you doing here, Mom?" I ask.

"What am *I* doing here? You have some nerve, young lady. I'm here to take you home," she yells, and I'm sure the people down the street can hear her.

"This is my home," I say, not recognizing my own voice.

"It sure isn't. Just because you left home without a word doesn't make this your home."

I've never seen my mom so angry before. She has always been the composed woman. Never have I seen her raise her voice or get angry.

"Maybe we should have this conversation in private, not where there are ears everywhere," Samuel mummers.

He's right. If we continue to have this conversation in the middle of the street, people will be drawn in by the spectacle and will start to talk.

"There is no we. This is a conversation between me and my daughter and has nothing to do with you," she snarls. She really doesn't like Samuel, and that breaks my heart.

"Mom…" I try to intervene, but Samuel holds up a hand to stop me.

"With all due respect, anything that concerns your daughter concerns me if she wants it to." He towers over her, but my mother stands her ground, not backing down.

"And why should it concern you? You are probably a pedophile, grooming her."

"Mother!" I yell at her.

"You know nothing about me or our relationship."

"I wonder what the police will have to say about you being with such a young girl." She won't stop. She will continue to spit out hate, and I won't have that.

"Enough! You will not speak to him like that. Like he said, you know nothing about him or our relationship. I'm not a child, Mother. I'm twenty-one. I'm allowed to make the choices I want." I'm mad, angry she would accuse him of such a thing. I can't take this anymore.

I turn to Samuel, whose eyes are filled with anger, and try

to diffuse the situation. "I'm going to take my mom to my apartment. Go home; I'll call you later."

"Zoey." He doesn't like the idea, but he has to let me do this.

"Please, Samuel," I beg. This will be the only way to calm down my mother.

Questions swim in his eyes, but he finally nods.

"I'll be at the store. We'll talk when you have everything handled," he says, leaning in to give me a kiss on the cheek. When he pulls back, he gives me a small smile before turning, glaring at my mother and walking down to the bookstore.

God, how I wish I could go with him.

But I have to be a big girl and talk to my mother without any interruptions.

"Let's go," I say to her, waving in the direction of my apartment. My mother follows me with her luggage in tow.

We walk in silence, and when we make it to my apartment, I can't help but think I might have to give up Matias and Samuel.

I don't know if I can do that.

No matter what my mother has to say.

CHAPTER 13

MATHIAS

’m about to cross the county line when my phone starts to ring. I see on the car display that it's Samuel, and I answer immediately. He would never call me like this unless something is wrong.

"What's going on?" I ask instead of a greeting.

He lets out a sigh before he answers. "Well, Zoey's mother is in town."

"Okay?" Why is her mother being in town a big deal?

"Yeah, and from just a few minutes with her, I got the impression Zoey didn't tell her where she was, and I was called a pedophile."

"What?!" My brother is a lot of things, but never a fucking pedophile.

"Yeah. According to her, I might be grooming her daughter."

"Zoey is twenty-one years old," I tell him. What the fuck is happening right now?

I leave for a few hours, and all shit breaks loose.

"Fuck," I say. I rack my brain for any other words, but I can't come up with any. "Where Zoey now?" I can't help but wonder if she's about to leave Crystal Springs with her mother.

"At her apartment with her mom. We had gone to dinner and were walking back to the store when she confronted us. I suggested it would be best to have whatever conversation that needed to be had in private."

Fuck. This lady called him a pedophile in public? Pinche Vieja.

"Why aren't you with her?"

"Because Zoey asked me to give them some time. So, I came to the store to wait for her to call me."

Shit show, I'm telling you.

I let out a sigh. "Okay, I will be there in about fifteen."

"Sounds good," he says before hanging up.

I was having a good day. I woke up with my girl at my side, naked, no less, and I'm coming off a good meeting with the small press. I was just going to go home, eat dinner, and maybe get lost in Zoey for the rest of the night.

That was the plan, but this shit had to come and ruin it.

About twenty minutes after ending the call, I pull into the bookstore parking lot and make my way inside. I find Samuel in the back chair, the one Zoey loves so much, drinking from a tumbler filled with amber liquid. Fucker is bringing out the hard stuff.

"Anything?" I ask.

He shakes his head. "Nope. Still waiting," he says, taking a drink.

"Did Zoey really not tell her mom she was moving here?" I ask, perching on a nearby stool.

"That's what I got from the conversation. According to her mother, she left without a word," Samuel says.

"But why?" I'm trying to wrap my head around why she would just leave home like that, but I can't come up with anything.

"From what she told me, she lived a very sheltered life and came to Crystal Springs to see what the world had to offer. She most likely didn't want her mom to stop her from doing that."

Well, fuck. I guess Zoey is a lot more adventurous than we thought.

After a few silent minutes, I grow restless. I need to know she's okay. I need to know she isn't going to pack her bags and leave us.

"I'm heading over there," I say, getting up.

"And do what?" my brother says, following my lead.

"I don't know. See what the fuck is going on? Convince her mother her daughter is in a good place here in California? I don't know," I say, extending my arms in frustration.

I know Samuel feels the same way I do, and if it wasn't for Zoey asking for some time, he would have been in that apartment with her.

He gives me a curt nod and heads for the door. "Let's go."

There is a slight chance that things are about to get uglier.

CHAPTER 14

Zoey

$\mathscr{A}$ disgrace.

Ruining the family name.

A hussy.

Those are all words my mom uses to describe my actions as soon as the apartment door closes behind us.

A disgrace because I left my family home without permission. A runaway.

Can you still be considered a runaway when you are legally an adult and have a way to support yourself?

The ruining the family name part ties into being called a hussy. According to my mother, I'm a little hussy because I'm in cahoots with an older man, and since I'm a hussy, I'm ruining her family name.

What would the people back home say when they find out her daughter is being courted by someone twice her age?

I tried to say there is only a twelve year age difference between me and Samuel, but it was pointless.

I wonder what she would say if I told her that not only am I in 'cahoots' with one older man, but two?

Maybe then, she will say I'm a slut or skank.

We've been in my apartment for a good twenty minutes, and all she has done is lecture me. I can't even get a word in, and I'm tired of it.

"Mom!" I yell, and finally, she stops talking.

You know that saying, if looks could kill? That saying would apply to the look she's giving her right now.

I raised my voice at her, something I have never done.

"How did you find me?" I asked, my voice a lot more leveled.

She squares her shoulders and meets my eyes straight on. "I got a notification from the bank saying you had successfully changed your address."

The things my mother does blows my mind. You would think that, in your twenties, your parents would no longer meddle in your life like this. I understand checking my bank accounts when I'm thirteen, but at this age? It's a little much.

"You have no right to do that," I say, already losing the effort to fight her.

"Yes, I do. You're my daughter, and I need to protect you from the evils of this world. I will start by taking you back home and away from this place."

"No." I stand my ground.

"What do you mean, 'no'?" She raises her eyebrows, questioning me yet again.

"I mean no. I'm not going back home. I like it here. I want

to build a life here; I am building a life here. No way in hell am I going to go back to West Virginia."

My mother gasps at the word hell. "Who are you, and what have you done with my daughter? Never would she say that word."

I can't help but roll my eyes. "She grew up, Mom. She discovered a new world, one she is happy with."

"You will be happy at home."

"No, I won't."

"Is this about *that* man? Is he manipulating you? Is that why you want to stay here so badly?" Her face contorts with disgust when she says *that man.*

I hate that she is talking about Samuel like that.

"You don't know a thing about him. He's not the type of person you think he is. He is good, and he is good to me. And yes, he is part of the reason I want to stay. The other part is that I really like it here. I can see myself building a life here."

I don't tell her I see building a life with not only Samuel, but also with Matias.

"He's taking advantage of you," she growls, and I shake his head.

"He's not." We've only been together for a few weeks, but I'm already falling for both brothers. I can already see myself loving them with everything I have.

Before I can say anything else, there's a knock at the door.

I don't get visitors, so the only people it could be are Matias or Samuel. I sigh; I knew Samuel wouldn't stay at the store, I just didn't think he would come knocking so soon.

Shaking my head, I turn away from my mother and go to the door. When I open it, I'm a little surprised to see both

Matias and Samuel standing there. I thought Mat would be back later tonight.

"Hi," I say to them, holding the door close, shielding my mother. She will surely go off if she sees Samuel.

"We wanted to make sure everything was okay," Matias says, sticking his hands in his pockets.

I nod to them, not saying anything.

"Zoey…" Samuel says, raising an eyebrow.

"Who is at the door, Zoey?" my mom asks from behind me.

I know she heard their voices, so I know better than to lie to her. If I lie right now, there's going to be another argument about how I've lost all respect for her.

With a sigh, I open the door wider and show my mother who's at the door.

Her hand goes to her chest in surprise when she sees it's Samuel.

"There's two of them," she gasps, her eyes jumping between the brothers.

"Yes, Mother, there are two of them, and guess what? I'm with both of them," I say before I can stop myself.

Holy crap. Did I just tell my mother I'm with two men?

By the look on her face, I did. I really told her that.

"Excuse me?" Her eyes look like they are going to pop out of her head.

"I, um…" What do I say? No, I didn't mean to say that? I'm not really with both of them? Nope. I'm not going to lie, and I won't talk down about my relationships.

No comprehendible words leave my mouth, and my mom beelines it to the twins.

"I don't know what kind of sick freaks you two are, but

you will not lay another hand on my daughter ever again. I should have you arrested for manipulating her. It makes me sick," she spits at them, and she's getting ready to slap both of them, but I stop her before she can swing.

"Mom, stop!" I yell.

"No. Pack your things. I'm getting out of this place!" she says, looking around before heading to my dresser and taking out all my clothes.

"Mom!"

Before I can say anything else, my mom marches over to me and slaps me across the face. My hand goes straight to my cheek, feeling the throbbing against my fingertips. My mother has never hit me before.

"That's enough." Samuel steps between me and my mother while Matias takes me in his arms.

"You don't get to tell me what to do, you filthy pig," my mom says to him, not caring that he's so much bigger than her. Samuel would never hurt her—he would never hurt anyone—but he does terrify people.

"With all the respect in the world, your daughter is an adult and of consenting age. She can do anything she damn well pleases. She doesn't have to ask your permission, whether that be to move here or to start a relationship with two grown adults. Those are her choices, and they have nothing to do with you."

"You have no right to talk to me like this," my mother snarls, stepping closer to Samuel.

"And you have no right to speak to the love of my life like that or lay a hand on her, mother or not. No one should be treated that way. You're just a cold, sadistic bitch who wants to control everything," Samuel grits out, standing his ground.

"Samuel..." Matias warns, which has Samuel turning around and taking me from Matias' arms, wiping the tears away.

"Look, Mrs. Thomas, I know this is unconventional. Yes, she is only twenty-one, and we're in our thirties, but my brother and I love your daughter. We would do anything for her. We will treat her with respect and give her all the love in the world. You spewing hate hurts her more than helps her. You should be proud she wants to explore the world instead of dragging her down. If anyone is in the wrong, it's you, not Zoey."

I stand there with Samuel's arms around me, watching Matias lecture my mother. She just stands there looking at him, trying to stand her ground, but from the looks of things, she is failing.

She squares her shoulders and walks past Matias to stand in front of me. I sink deeper into Samuel's arms, fearing she might slap me again.

"Is this what you want?" she says through clenched teeth, eyebrows bunched together.

I nod slowly. "I want to stay here, with Samuel and Matias. I love them just as much as they love me," I whisper.

"If you stay, you will not be welcomed back home," she tells me. I knew my mother would hate me for my decisions, but never did I think she would be this way. I never thought she would disown me like this.

I swallow the lump in my throat, detangle myself from Samuel, and face my mother straight on.

There are tears forming in my eyes, but I'm able to get the words out.

"I'm sorry, Mom, but I'm staying here. Where I belong."

There is no sadness in her face—just anger, pure anger.

With a curt nod, she walks around me and leaves the apartment without another glance.

I want to call after her, scream at her how sorry I am and how I wish she could accept my decision, but I don't. Nothing I say will change the situation.

As I watch her leave, the tears come faster, until I can't take them anymore and fall to my knees from all the emotional pain.

A set of arms picks me up, and then another set wraps around me when I'm laid on the bed.

They hold me while I cry all the pain away.

When the only sound that fills the room is my crying, I say the words I need to say.

"Matias. Samuel."

"What is it, cariño?" Samuel asks.

"I love you."

CHAPTER 15

SAMUEL

I've never wanted to take someone else's pain away like I want to take away Zoey's.

A part of my beautiful girl broke when her mother walked out on her. Never did I think the night would have escalated as it did.

There is a part of me that wants to apologize to Zoey for even coming to the apartment. We should have stayed at the bookstore and let her handle her mother on her own. But Matias and I are stupid, and we came knocking at her door anyway.

Now, we are lying with her in our arms as she cries her eyes out. I don't know how long we have been like this, but if she needs to, I will be here all night for her, and I know my brother would do the same.

Zoey shifts in our arms. "Matias. Samuel." I hear the pain in her voice.

"What is it, cariño?" I ask her. I would give her the moon right now if she asked for it.

"I love you."

Three glorious words I never thought I would ever hear coming from her lips.

Earlier, when we were discussing with her mother, the words slipped out of our mouths, but we meant them. Now, she is gifting us those words herself.

I look over at Matias, and his eyes meet mine. Silently, we both turn to face her, wiping the tears from her beautiful face.

"I love you too," we both say at the same time. Sometimes, being a twin has its benefits.

We lean forward and place kisses along her neck, her cheek, and Zoey lets out a contented sigh. My brother and I have a silent understanding that we are going to make Zoey feel better and forget about what just occurred with her mother.

Matias takes her lips, and I make my way down her body, savoring every inch of her I can.

Pushing up her shirt, I kiss her stomach, and I continue pushing the fabric covering her up and away until I reach her tits.

"Such glorious tits," I muse before I unclasp her bra and take one of her breasts in my mouth, swirling my tongue along her nipple before I move on to the other one.

Zoey lets out a moan, telling me she is enjoying what I'm doing to her body.

I can mark her tits as mine all fucking day, but tonight, I want to make her feel good. I want her to feel things she has never felt before.

Continuing down her body, I strip off her jeans, then the

leggings she wore under to battle the cold, while Matias strips her of her shirt and bra, marveling at her tits.

They are glorious tits, and we both love them.

Once she is bare from the waist down, I get situated between her thighs and devour her pussy in the way I know she likes.

The thing about having sex with someone on a regular basis—you learn what they prefer and what they hate. I have become fortunate to know exactly what Zoey likes when it comes to her pussy being eaten. A loud moan fills the room when my tongue flattens against her lips.

"Such a little slut, huh? You love it when he eats your pussy." Zoey must have nodded at Matias' statement, because he says, "Say the words, baby. Say how much you love it when Sam eats your pussy."

"I love it when he eats my pussy," she pants.

"Good girl," he says before I hear a zipper being pulled down.

"I think tonight might be the night," I say against Zoey's mound. I know my brother knows what I'm getting at. I don't need to say the words.

"Yeah?" he asks, making sure I'm serious about this.

"Yeah," I say right before I lick Zoey, clit to asshole, getting her ready for what we have in mind.

Fuck.

Just the thought of it makes my cock so unbearably hard, I have to press it against the mattress to relieve some of the discomfort.

Zoey grinds herself against my face, and I can't help but smile at her greediness.

"Greedy girl, always wanting to get there faster."

"I need to come," she pants, and I look to find she has Matias' dick in her hands, pumping him.

"And you will—when I say you can." I suck her clit before I sit up and position myself so my lips are close to hers, my hands rubbing circles around her little bundle of nerves.

"Samuel," she whines, and I take some of the frustration away by sliding two fingers into her.

"Is this what you want?" I say against her lips as I thrust in and out of her. "Do you want to come on my fingers, baby?

I pick up the pace, touching her g-spot and hooking my fingers.

Zoey nods rapidly, "Yes."

"Good little slut," Matias croons while he pulls and twists her nipples.

I hook my fingers in her again and start moving faster. Zoey starts to tremble, her body shaking with the intensity.

"Fuck!" she yells out, her release taking over, coating not only my fingers but my whole hand. She tightens even more around me, and I don't stop until she lets out a scream of pleasure and explodes all over the bed.

As she comes down, I slip my fingers out of her and slap her pussy, spreading her release.

"She's ready," I tell Matias, and a devilish smirk takes over his face.

He nods and quickly rids himself of all clothing before situating himself so Zoey is above him, her luscious ass facing me.

We have been prepping her body for this moment. We knew a time would come when we would both want to take her at the same time, so we've been trying to help her get used to the sensation.

Our fingers and some toys have been our arsenal, but tonight, we change that.

After rolling on a condom, Matias she slides her down his cock.

God, Zoey looks gorgeous like this, with a cock inside her and her ass up, waiting for me to take it.

Zoey starts riding Matias, forgetting that she just came not even a minute ago.

I undress before climbing on the bed again, taking my place behind her.

"That's it. Ride his cock like a good girl," I say, sliding on a condom of my own and grabbing the globes of her ass. I run a finger along her ass crack, and when I press it against her tight hole, she lets out a moan.

"This is going to sting, baby. It might be a lot more pressure than what you experienced during your first time. Just relax and let us take care of you," I say, rubbing small circles along her back.

"Take a deep breath, tesoro. Everything will be alright," Matias says, taking her face in his hands and kissing her senseless.

While he's kissing her, I slide my finger into her hole, stretching her so she can take my cock.

As the kiss intensifies, Zoey becomes more relaxed, so I pull replace my finger with the tip of my cock at her opening.

She feels me and pulls away from my brother, turning to look at me.

"I'm ready," she pants.

At her words, I slowly slide my cock deeper into her, feeling her tightness around me. It's such a surreal feeling. She is so tight, it feels like she is going to cut my dick off, but it feels fucking amazing.

"Fuck," I pant as I continue to slide into her.

"Are you okay?" Matias asks her.

"Yes," she groans; I really wish I could see her face right about now. "It's just a lot of pressure. I think once you two start moving, I will be okay."

I can hear the strain in her voice.

"Start moving," I say to Matias once I'm seated in Zoey.

He starts to move, and after a few seconds, I follow suit.

She is so much tighter like this, with two cocks in her. I don't think any of us will be lasting long.

"Holy shit." Matias lets out as he pounds into Zoey from below, and I agree with him. Holy shit.

Zoey lets out moan after moan, a sound I want to hear for the rest of my life.

"I'm going to come," she yells out.

"Come, baby. Give us everything you have." I give her ass a slap and continue to slide in and out of her tight hole.

"Fuck, you look so fucking beautiful with two cocks in you. How good does it feel, baby?" Matias gets out through a moan.

"So good. So, so good," Zoey is able to get out before her whole body starts to shake and she succumbs to her orgasm. The sensation of her coming is enough for me to explode, and I load the condom with every last drop I have.

Matias is close behind me.

"So fucking good," I groan when I pull out of Zoey and see her hole puckering and swollen. Such a beautiful sight. I lean forward and press a few kisses on her hole to relieve some of the pain she must be feeling.

I head to the bathroom to get a washcloth, and when I come back out, Zoey has dislodged herself from Matias and is cuddled up into his side.

Opening her legs, I clean her up before climbing on the bed and situating myself on Zoey's other side.

As she lays in our arms for the second time tonight, I can't help think that as I grow old, this is what I want my life to be.

I want Zoey in my life, at my side, driving me wild with her body and her need to explore. And yes, sharing her with my brother.

This is an unconventional situation like we told her mom, but it works for us. This is how we're supposed to play out, the three of us together, *happy*.

Ever since Zoey came into town, I have always pictured sharing her with my brother. At the time, it was just about the sexual satisfaction, but now, weeks later, it has grown into a lot more.

And I'm glad it did.

I'm glad Zoey came into our lives and changed it for the better.

Offering her a job was the best decision I have made, and when it comes to her, I hope I keep making them. That we both do.

Matias and I will take care of Zoey, and we will give her anything and everything she wants.

We love her, and we won't give her up. If she wants to step away, we will let her, but for now, she's ours, and there is no way in fucking hell we are going to let her go.

Zoey is our everything and hopefully one day, we will be able to show her just that.

CHAPTER 16

Matias

This is probably the worst decision I have made in a long time. There is no reason for me to be here. The only reason I am is because I love Zoey and want her to be happy.

Seeing what her mother's actions did to her, I wanted to fix it. I wanted to go after her mother and bring her back so she could apologize to her daughter.

I didn't.

Instead, Samuel and I consoled her in the best way we could. We held her and let her forget the night with our bodies.

We were connected in ways I could never explain, and it felt amazing. If Zoey lets us, I know my brother and I could worship her body every single night for the rest of our lives.

I take a sip of my coffee and wait for her to arrive at the bus stop.

Early this morning, I set out to find Zoey's mother. Samuel heard me, and when I told him what I was doing, he looked at the woman sleeping in the bed next to him and nodded for me to go.

He wants the same thing as me, and he will try his damn hardest to give it to her.

So, here I am, sitting on a bench with a coffee in my hand on a cold morning, waiting for Mrs. Thomas to arrive for her bus ride home.

It wasn't hard to find out when she was leaving; all it took one phone call to the inn in town, and I had all the information I needed.

Now, it's just a waiting game for her to show up. Looking at the time on my phone, I see the bus is set to arrive in a few minutes, so that means Mrs. Thomas will get here any minute now.

And sure enough, within a minute, I hear luggage being dragged across the concrete, heading in my direction.

I look up, and right away, I'm met with the same pair of eyes I love so much. I didn't notice it last night, but Zoey and her mother look so much alike, the resemblance is uncanny.

"Good morning, Mrs. Thomas," I say, announcing my presence.

Right away, she looks over at me and gives me the dirtiest look she can muster.

I get it, I do. I'm the bad guy in this scenario for sexually exploiting her daughter. But that isn't what's happening us.

"I have nothing to say to you," she spits as she walks past me. I get up and stupidly follow.

"Then maybe you will be opened to listening," I say to her as she continues to walk away.

"And what exactly would I be listening to? Are you going to tell me all about how what you're doing to my daughter is normal?" she spits without even turning to face me.

And here I thought she didn't have anything to say.

"I just wanted to say I know you don't approve of our relationship with your daughter. But we do really love her, and we want her to be happy. We will try our hardest to make that happen. So, I wanted to meet with you this morning before you head home to tell you that even though you don't approve, your daughter will be in good hands. Know we will take care of her to best we can, and we will never voluntarily hurt her."

This makes her stop. For a few minutes, she just stands there in the middle of the sidewalk, probably running my words through her head.

Everything is the truth, every last word, and if she doesn't accept that, then she is just hurting herself more.

"All I ever wanted was to protect my daughter from the same world that dragged me through the mud. I didn't want her to experience the same things I did. Never did I think I might have been doing it wrong or that she wouldn't want it." She breaks the silence, finally turning to look at me.

I nod. "I get that I do, but sometimes, you have to look at the broader picture and ask yourself if you are going about it the right way."

She nods. "Never did I think she would find herself in the arms of a man states away from me, let alone two. How old are you anyway?" There is no judgment in her tone, that much I can tell.

"Thirty-three, but age is just a number. Yes, we are older than her, but we don't look at it that way. We don't see her as a little girl. We see her as a woman who has a whole life ahead of her."

She nods again, not looking up at me. "I can't accept this, not right now. Give me some time to process everything, and maybe I will get the courage to come back here and really talk to my daughter."

"I think she would like that."

The bus pulls into the station, and Mrs. Thomas sets her shoulders back before she turns to face me head on.

"Take care of my daughter. Love her and give her the best life you can," she tells me, and from where I'm standing, I spot tears forming in her eyes.

I nod. "We will."

With a small smile in my direction, she turns and gets on the bus.

I stand there until the bus leaves and then head back to Zoey's place, grabbing breakfast along the way. When I walk inside, I find the two of them cuddled up in bed, watching tv.

"Where did you go?" Zoey asks when I head to her kitchen.

"Just went to get some breakfast," I tell her with a smile. She untangles herself from Samuel to place a kiss on my lips.

"Good morning," she says with a bright smile.

"Good morning, mi mujer hermosa."

She takes the food and gets plates out so we can eat. Samuel joins us, clapping me on the shoulder, silently asking if everything is good.

I nod. Everything is okay for now.

Soon, the three of us are having breakfast, enjoying each other's company and talking about a bunch of random shit.

This is what has been missing in our lives.

Zoey.

She gives our lives more stability, and not just something on repeat. She brings a brightness to our world and makes us want things we've never wanted before.

With her, we want the seriousness, the future, the happily ever after shit. She makes us want it all.

I thought, coming to Crystal Springs all those years ago, that Booked was going to be my solace, but what I didn't know was that my solace would come much later, in the form of a woman with blonde hair and eyes that look like the moon. In such a short time, she has become our everything.

Only time will tell if the two of us will be able to give her everything in return.

EPILOGUE

EIGHT YEARS LATER

ZOEY

"Take my cock, tesoro. Take it like you know how to do so well."

"Fuck her harder, you asshole. Make her pussy drip."

Matias' fingers dig into my hips as he pounds his thick cock into me. His fingers digging into my hips feel amazing, but I don't know if it compares to how Samuel's fingers feel as they pull my hair and brings my mouth closer to him. I love the feeling of one cock in my mouth and the other in my pussy.

I love it even more when they take my pussy and my tight asshole.

I love everything they do to my body.

With a moan, I slip Samuel's cock out of my mouth and

give him a few strokes with my hand. "I'm going to come," I announce.

"Fuck." Matias groans, slapping my ass and digging his nails deeper into my skin.

Samuel grabs me by the hair, brings his cock back to my face and slapping my cheek with it.

"You going to come on my cock? ¿Me vas a chupar?" I nod at Samuel's words. "Fuck, cariño. And while you come, are you going to swallow me down your throat?" I nod again.

"Such a dirty woman," Matias says with another grunt.

"Our dirty woman," Samuel declares, stroking my cheek before fucking my mouth. "Fill her up, hermano. Give her everything you have."

I don't know how much I can handle. There are tears rolling down my cheeks from the way Samuel is fucking my mouth, and my body feels on fire with the way Matias is fucking my pussy.

It's too much.

I can't handle it anymore; I need a release.

Letting out a yell—as much of a yell as I can muster with Samuel's cock in my mouth—I explode around Matias.

"Fuck, yes. That's it, tesoro. Coat my fucking cock. Fuck." With just one more thrust, Matias is coming, filling me to the point that I know his release will be rolling down my thighs.

Samuel is close behind his brother, filling my mouth, and I swallow every drop.

"Mm, cariño, you sure know how to drain us," Samuel murmurs as he strokes my cheeks, ridding them of the tears that escaped.

I give him a smile, and he leans down to kiss me on the

lips. At the same time, I feel Matias trailing kisses along my back.

I absolutely love it when they're animalistic with me one minute and then sweet as they can be, worshipping my body as a temple.

They treat me like a queen, and they have from our very first time.

It has been eight years since I walked into the bookstore, eight years since my heart exploded for these two sexy men.

Matias and Samuel have become my everything, and I try to show them every single day just how much they mean to me.

In the last eight years, we've been able to add on to our house and make it feel more like a home. Each of us has a room, and, ninety nine percent of the time, we all sleep in my room, which has the biggest bed to accommodate all of us. Still, even though I love being shared, there are moments I like to spend time with each of them separately. It's not often, but it does happen, and it's good for us.

If you're thinking they might get jealous about me spending more time with the other brother, you're wrong. As long as I'm taken care of, they are happy. They are only ever jealous when an outsider tries to hit on me; then, their possessive sides come out to play.

Those nights are my favorite, because the things they do to me are from romance novels. I can't walk for days after, and I fucking love it. Matias dislodges himself and positions me so I'm lying down. He gives me a passionate kiss and then gets situated with his chest to my back.

Samuel lays down next to me, but instead of facing me and

his brother, he lays on his back, grabs my hand, and puts it on his stomach. My legs automatically tangle with his.

I don't know how long we lay there before Matias speaks. "Do you think that was the one?"

"I sure fucking hope so," Samuel growls, and I can't help but giggle into his chest.

Before I can even respond, the baby monitor goes off— the baby is awake and hungry.

"Duty calls," I say, untangling myself from my men, getting dressed, and heading down the hall.

Right after Thanksgiving two years ago, I found out I was pregnant, and gave Samuel and Matias the surprise on Noche Buena. I was a little nervous about how they would react, especially since I will never know who the father is, but, when I told them, they were both ecstatic.

They didn't care who the father was—they were just over the moon I was pregnant.

For the next nine months, they read every baby book they could and got the house ready. Some of those extra rooms we added are for that very reason.

We needed room for the baby and all the other babies Samuel and Matias were determined to have. According to them, they'll try and get me pregnant however many times I allow. And for right now, I'm okay with that.

I walk into our son's room and find him setting up, eyes filled with wonder.

At eight months old, my little boy is getting so big.

"Hi, baby boy. Did Mami and Papis wake you?" I lift him from his crib and head to the rocking chair to feed him. Next month, he will be on the bottle, so until then, I will cherish these moments.

Gael is the perfect combination of me and his fathers, a beautiful baby. I hear footsteps nearing the room, and when I look up, I see my two gorgeous men standing in the doorway.

"That's the most beautiful sight I have ever seen," Samuel says, crossing his arms across his chest.

"I have to agree," Matias says with a nod, and I can't help but smile.

I can't believe this is my life. I can't believe a spur of the moment decision to move to a small town in the California mountains has led to this.

Never did I think walking into that little bookstore would lead to me, meeting the loves of my life, and holding their child.

They love me unconditionally.

They fuck me uncontrollably.

And I can't believe they're mine.

THE END.

ACKNOWLEDGMENTS

Five years ago, I never thought that this book will ever see the light of day again, but I was wrong and here it is. Tweaks were made and now this story is better than ever.

When I first wrote it, I wanted to step out of my comfort zone and write something a little more spicier than what I'm used to and I think it works.

Thank you for giving it a shot. I hope you enjoyed it.

Thank you to Samantha and Mel at Ink and Velvet for brining the characters to life.

Thank you to Alexa at The Fiction Fix for helping me edit this baddie in a time crunch

Thank you to Ellie at My Brother's Editor for the proof and sticking with me through the years.

Thank you to you reader for reading my words and loving my characters so that I can continue writing. I will be thanking you in every life time .

Now onto the next one!

Powerful Deception

Fake Love

Salutis Meae

Booked For The Winter

Jocelyne Soto is an independent author living in California. She loves reading romance and discovering new authors. She comes from a big Mexican family, and with it comes a love for all things family and food.
Jocelyne has a love for her mom's coffee and writing. In her free time, you can find her reading a romance novel on her kindle while writing heartwarming and chaotic romance stories in between. From sport romance to dark romance, there is no limit as to the type of stories that will come to Jocelyne's mind.

Check out her website for ways to connect with Jocelyne!
www.jocelynesoto.com

instagram.com/authorjocelynesoto
tiktok.com/@authorjocelynesoto
facebook.com/authorjocelynesoto
threads.com/@authorjocelynesoto

JOIN MY READER GROUP

Join my ever-growing Facebook Group. You get first looks,
sneak peeks and giveaways!

NEWSLETTER

Sign up for my Newsletter!
You will get notified when there are new
releases to look out for, giveaways and more!

www.ingramcontent.com/pod-product-compliance
Lightning Source LLC
Chambersburg PA
CBHW021736190726
48288CB00009B/3067